SPORTS LOVERS

FRIENDSHIP CHRONICLES 7

SHELLEY MUNRO

MUNRO PRESS

Sports Lovers

Copyright © 2023 by Shelley Munro

Print ISBN: 978-1-99-106338-0
Digital ISBN: 978-0-9951395-9-6

Editor: Evil Eye Editing

Cover: Kim Killion, The Killion Group, Inc.

Munro Press, New Zealand.

First Munro Press electronic publication October 2021

First Munro Press print publication August 2023

DEDICATION

For Paul, my partner in crime and fellow adventurer.

"I travel because I'd rather look back at my life, saying 'I
can't believe I did that' instead of 'if only I had'."
— Florine Bos

INTRODUCTION

AMBITION TRUMPS LOVE AND romance, doesn't it?

Holly sucks when it comes to choosing the perfect man, and at three duds for three, she's turning her back on the dating game. Instead, she'll embrace ambition, concentrate on her favored sport and her promise to her deceased mother—she'll do her utmost to earn a place in New Zealand's netball team, the Silver Ferns.

Burned by a rough divorce, rugby player Angus isn't interested in anything but casual relationships. That's until he meets Holly. With common mindsets, they're perfect together, but Holly is running scared and refuses to see their potential.

Given his public persona, wooing isn't something Angus usually needs to practice. With Holly, he's willing to work for each passionate kiss. If only the real world and their romantic histories didn't keep creating roadblocks...

You'll love this sports romance because it contains a talented but man-shy heroine, an alpha hero with a playboy reputation, their tentative friendship, and enough exes coming out of the woodwork to create their own sports team. Go, Holly! Go, Angus!

NOTE TO READERS

THE SPORT OF NETBALL has a special place in my heart since I played the game during my school years and until my husband and I went overseas when I was in my early twenties. Games took place on Saturdays during the winter, while training occurred after school. I loved the game and played on the defensive end of the court since I was always taller than my friends. Both of my knees bear scars from falls because the surface we played on was unforgiving.

While netball might not be familiar to those in the United States, it has its roots in 1891 Springfield, Massachusetts, and basketball. The game arrived in the United Kingdom in 1895 and spread to countries like Australia, New Zealand, and the West Indies.

These days, netball is one of the sports played during the Commonwealth Games. It's a popular sport, and young girls still play netball on winter Saturday mornings as I did.

For those interested in learning more about the game and its rules, visit NZ Netball. (www.netballnz.co.nz)

1

HER SISTER'S DATE

HOLLY BLACKWOOD STRAIGHTENED FROM her slouch on the faded but comfy green chair. She nailed her older half-sister with a scowl. "No way are you fixing me up with a blind date. Besides, I have training tomorrow morning. I want to rest tonight."

Brooke screwed up her pixy nose. She paced back and forth in front of the TV, her current fruity perfume reminding Holly of fresh pears wafting in the air. "Are you sure?"

"Yes." Holly waved the TV remote in emphasis. "Positive."

"But Angus has friends—an entire rugby team of them."

Holly scowled harder and fervently wished she hadn't answered the apartment door when her sister had shrieked that she'd left her key at work. It was just after six, and she was knackered, her muscles throbbing from fatigue. Their coach had pushed them at this afternoon's netball training, and she was still recovering from the taxing session.

"What?" Brooke prodded when Holly remained silent. She released her blonde hair from its braid and finger-combed the long locks while regarding Holly with expectation. "I'm sure Angus wouldn't mind setting you up with one of his friends."

"No! I'm done with rugby players." Bother, all she'd wanted was to watch a reality show and chill. "All right. *All right.* I'll go to your party, but I don't need to hang off a man's arm while I'm there. I can stand on my own." Holly waggled a foot in her sister's direction, offering positive size eleven proof of her ability to remain upright without aid. "I have plenty of grip on the ground."

They took a moment to stare at Holly's foot. It was long and narrow and sported a red-and-white striped sock. Her big toe stuck through a hole, showcasing her aquamarine nail. She tried to recall when she'd applied the polish. A month ago or longer?

Brooke sniffed in obvious disapproval. "I'll give you a pedicure tomorrow."

"Maybe I'll stay at home," Holly said quickly. "To redo my nails." She should resent her older sister, a petite and shapely blonde with her bubbly manner. Brooke never had trouble making friends—the stereotypical social butterfly.

"No," Brooke said, emphatic. "You're turning into a hermit. Work and netball training. That's all you do. *Every day of the week*. Please socialize, or I'll have to field questions about your passing. You need to get over your trust issues. Not everyone is like that arsehole Craig."

Well, heck, that hadn't worked. Not that she'd expected Brooke to cave. "I've said I'd attend the party, and I will, but I'm not going on a date with anyone. My energy levels aren't up to handling pawing hands or coping with a man who expects sex in exchange for his company. The social chitchat and getting-to-know-you stuff are stressful enough." Holly gave a theatrical shudder, which was only half pretense. Social occasions and all that sexual maneuvering brought her out in hives. She preferred straight talk and honesty every time.

"You'd mellow if you got some," Brooke shot back.

"That's working out well for you." *Aw, crap.* She regretted the unthinking words the instant they left her mouth. "I'm sorry, Brooke. I didn't mean—"

Brooke held up her hand, her expression no longer transparent and teasing. "Sebastian and I are over, and I refuse to discuss him. Tonight, I intend to enjoy Angus's company, and if we get on okay, a little recreational sex is just the thing to dropkick Seb to the past."

Holly kept her comments behind sealed lips. Brooke and Sebastian regularly called it quits, a scene replayed since their first date at high school. She'd given up trying to understand the dynamics of their relationship.

"What should I wear?" she asked in an about-face.

It was the perfect distraction. Brooke worked part-time on the makeup counter of an Auckland department store while completing her beauty therapy studies. During the rugby season, she was on the cheerleading squad for the Auckland Dragons. Her sister adored fashion.

"Let's check your wardrobe."

Holly heaved herself off the chair with a groan and limped after Brooke as her sister headed to the double bedroom they shared in their Newmarket apartment. Brooke flung open the wardrobe door. Holly's half was sparse, with an emphasis on casual and comfortable. Sportswear.

Brooke rifled through Holly's clothes. "No. No. No. You'll have to borrow something of mine."

"What?" Holly's brows lifted. Although they were close in size, Holly had six inches on her sister at just under six feet. While the height gave her an advantage on the netball court, it didn't make borrowing Brooke's clothing easy.

Brooke frowned, then the lines magically cleared. "I have just the thing. I'll need to iron it first. You make dinner, and I'll sort us out in the clothes department."

Holly sighed and limped to the kitchen. She opened the fridge to study the contents before pulling out vegetables to make a stir-fry. Hopefully, the outfit her sister had in mind was at least decent and didn't show half her butt or expose most of her boobs. How soon could she escape this party? Sleep was what she craved, not a man or passionate sex.

How long was socially polite?

MUSIC BLARED, A BOUNCY pop tune filling every corner of the private room at the pub. Shouts and laughter carried to where Angus O'Neil sat at a secluded table with his date, the lighting low and intimate. The perfect setting.

But instead of getting to know Brooke during this first date, Angus couldn't keep his eyes off Brooke's sister, Holly Blackwood. The woman in her figure-hugging black camisole top and matching black mini skirt danced with abandon, her body moving to the beat. The blonde was tall with Vegas showgirl legs, her moves on the dancefloor attracting more than his attention.

Angus forced himself to glance away and take a sip of his beer, but his single-track mind kept yammering about her naked, those sexy limbs twined around his hips while he fucked her.

Then there was his second favorite fantasy. Holly on her knees with that decadent red-painted mouth stretched around his cock, her blue eyes trained on his face. Oh yeah, it had been a busy night in Fantasy Land.

A problem since he was here at the party with Holly's older sister.

But hell, the way Holly grooved on the dance floor gave a guy ideas.

His breath gusted out, and he shifted to ease the fit of his black trousers. While Brooke was a knockout, it had been Holly with her extra height who drew him. She'd grabbed his attention from their introduction with her incredible blue eyes and long honey-blonde hair. That hair he'd love to wrap around his fingers to control her mouth—

Mind out of the gutter, O'Neil.

He was here on a date with Holly's sister—half-sister according to Brooke. Other guys might consider ditching a woman and pursuing another—he'd seen them in action—but he wasn't that man.

Angus grabbed a bottle of beer and focused on the conversation around him. Sports-related since ninety-nine percent of the party attendees were part of the rugby scene—either player or cheerleader.

Brooke leaned closer. Her perfume was full of Oriental spices and reminded him of his grandmother's apple pie—a sophisticated version, of course. Her breath warmed his ear, and that pushed his mind toward satin sheets. To his shame, the petite and curvy blonde wasn't the woman spread-eagle and naked on the middle of the mattress in his daydream vision.

"I'm off to the restroom," Brooke told him.

She drew back, flashed him a flirtatious smile, and he nodded in acknowledgment.

As a newcomer to the Auckland Dragons, he found the crowd welcoming, and with sports in common, conversation flowed easily. Joking and laughter rang out from throats lubricated with drinks. The sense of a job well done permeated the room since the Dragons had beaten the top-ranked Crows in front of a home crowd earlier in the day.

"Great try, dude," a man he recognized as a prominent rugby league player said.

"Thanks." He'd dotted down after intercepting the ball and running almost the length of the field. "We had an excellent result today. It was a team effort."

Holly appeared flushed and attractive after dancing, her shiny blonde hair tousled and leading his thoughts straight to sex again. Was that how she'd look after lovemaking?

There was an empty seat beside him—Brooke's seat.

"Where's Brooke?" Holly visibly hesitated, studying him as if he might take a bite.

God, he'd love to suck her succulent flesh and leave a lover's mark. Heat rushed through him, leaving him almost dizzy after the redirection of blood to his groin. He shook himself back to the party. Damn, his mind sailed in one direction tonight. He had it bad. "She's gone to the restrooms. Take her seat. I'm sure she won't mind. Here's your drink. I've kept an eye on it for you."

After wavering for another beat, she dropped onto the wooden chair. Her weight shifted until she perched like a bird prepared to take off at the first hint of danger. Angus wanted to smile but worried he'd resemble the predator that stalked through his mind.

If anyone had informed him this morning he'd have an urgent and instant reaction to a woman, he would've called bullshit.

No denying it now. Her scent washed over him—an old-fashioned lavender with a hint of orange. Another interesting contrast between the sisters since Brooke's perfume reeked of sophistication.

Aware of his understated—okay, not so subtle observation—she swallowed and fanned her face. Without taking his attention from her, he handed over her wine. She took a healthy swig, knocking back the remains.

Her gaze darted to him, and she gave a breathless laugh. "It's hot on the dance floor."

Her chuckle, husky and low, rocked him and had his body reacting yet again. This time he was the one to swallow. "Want some of my beer?"

"Yuck, disgusting. Beer is only good for bread. My mother makes fantastic beer bread." She paused, took a quick breath, and Angus couldn't fail to notice the rise and fall of her breasts. "Ah...I hear the Dragons had a win today."

"Yeah." She was aware of him too. *Interesting.* "It's great

to have a win on the board after our last loss in Australia."
He didn't want to talk rugby, not when his curiosity
centered on learning more about Holly Blackwood. "Are
you a cheerleader like your sister?"

"Me?" Astonishment, chased swiftly by amusement,
sparkled in her blue eyes. A dimple flashed at the right
corner of her mouth, charming him. "No way."

"So, what do you do?"

"I work for a bank, and in my spare time, I play netball
for the Blue Dynamos."

Her words made him scrutinize her with even greater
interest. Everything he uncovered about her fascinated
him more. "How long have you been playing for them?"

"This is my first season." She flashed him a proud grin,
passion for her sport shining in her features. "Still can't
believe I made the squad. I have to keep pinching myself."

"What position do you play?"

"Defense—goal keep and goal defense mainly, but I've
played on the wing too."

He noted she relaxed once she talked about netball. "Are
you in the starting team?"

"I was last week." Her dimple blinked into prominence
again.

He nodded, understanding the thrill of making the top
team. "My sister used to play netball before she had kids.
She played at the attack end of the court—on the wing."

"You know netball?" Holly glanced at the table and

pointed at the jug of margarita mix and the half-full glass. "Is that Brooke's?"

"Yup. I don't know what's happened to her."

Not that he was worried about his date's absence. He was positive Brooke recognized the lack of spark between them too. While he liked Brooke and her open manner, they'd make much better friends than lovers.

Angus smiled at Holly and took pleasure in the slight widening of her blue eyes. "I used to watch my sister train. My rugby practice finished earlier than her netball, so I'd end up waiting. Let me see." He pretended to ponder when he knew the game backward. Knowledge of netball and attending a game or two worked great for a guy wanting to meet the opposite sex. All those short uniforms and long legs didn't hurt either. "There are seven players per team. The court is divided into thirds, and the object is to score the most goals. A goal is worth one point. Each player position is only allowed in part of the court, and the ball is thrown from player to player to travel the court. There—how'd I do?"

Holly sipped her sister's drink. "You do know more than the average person."

"That's what I've been telling you. When is your next game?"

"We have a game on Monday night. The coach picks on form every week. Hopefully, I've done enough to make the team."

A note of apprehension slipped into her expression, a feeling he understood all too well. No player showcased their skill by watching from the sideline. "How much training do you do?"

"I run every morning, and we have—" She glanced over his shoulder, her faint smile fading abruptly.

He followed her gaze and couldn't see anything to promote her reaction. "What's wrong?"

"Brooke is dancing with Sebastian."

"Who's Sebastian?"

"Brooke's ex. They broke up last week."

Angus twisted on his chair to face the dance floor. His brows rose. "They're not together anymore?" Brooke had plastered her body against the dude. As he and Holly watched, Brooke linked her hands behind Sebastian's neck, and the pair kissed.

"I don't believe it," Holly murmured. "She swore they were finished."

"It appears they've changed their minds." He kept his voice mild, not even minor annoyance making an appearance since inwardly he cheered.

Holly tensed and ripped her gaze off her sister to eye him. "You won't make a scene?" She swallowed the last of her sister's margarita and poured another glass.

"No, I'm gonna have another drink, and I might ask you to dance. And maybe we can stand as close as your sister and her...man," Angus said.

Her mouth rounded a little before she pressed her scarlet lips together again. "You want to dance with me?"

"Yes, after we have a drink. Would you like another glass of wine?"

"Why not?" Holly wrinkled her nose at her margarita. "I'll have a glass of sauvignon blanc, please."

"Be right back," Angus said, and giving in to temptation, he ran his fingers across the dimple near her mouth. Her skin was even silkier than he'd imagined, and her eyes turned big and wide at the intimacy. Grinning, he headed for the bar with real pep in his step.

She'd poured herself another margarita and consumed half of it before he returned. Her foot tapped to the beat of a recent pop song while she chatted with a giggly blonde.

Holly straightened, her expression wary. "Angus, this is Marcia. She's on the cheer squad with Brooke."

"Nice to meet you, Marcia." This awareness wasn't just him. Holly was conscious of him too and running scared. The thrill of the hunt simmered through Angus as he considered his next move.

"I saw you score your try this afternoon," Marcia said with a flirty giggle and a toss of her head. "You're talented. Oh, and I saw the article about you in the *Women's Daily*. Great pics."

"Thanks," Angus said and wished she'd go away. He wanted to talk with Holly. *Alone.* Hell, he wanted to whisk her back to his apartment and explore the chemistry that sizzled between them. They'd have coffee if Holly wanted, but he'd prefer her in his king-size bed, naked.

"Angus."

Angus glanced up to see his team captain.

"Hulme is here. I'll introduce you," the captain said. "It's good to meet the selectors in person."

Angus hesitated.

"Go ahead." Relief slid into Holly's eyes. "I'll be fine."

Boom! That was his ego popping. "Back in a minute," Angus said and took undue pleasure in the guardedness that slotted back into place on Holly Blackwood's face. The woman didn't know it, but she'd issued a silent dare.

Angus O'Neil didn't back away from challenges. He relished them.

Holly sat at the table, a smile fixed on her lips. All around her, men and women flirted, drank, and laughed. Whispered to each other. Touched each other in the dim-lit room. Marcia had hailed an acquaintance and moved off to flirt with the guy, leaving Holly by herself. She puffed out a breath, loneliness grabbing her by the throat.

Mostly, she was content with her single life, but occasionally the yearning for a warm body to slide against during the cold winter nights got to her. A man—a non-rugby playing one—would be nice, but the aggravation males brought with them made her hesitate.

If she'd had spare cash, she might've ordered a vibrator.

Glumly, Holly drank the wine Angus had bought for her. *Ooh*, some of the expensive stuff. She took another sip and savored the crisp notes of fruit and sunshine.

"Hi, beautiful. Would you like to dance?"

Holly squinted up at the man. Another rugby player, judging by his stocky build. The private room in the pub was lousy with them.

"I promised I'd keep our seats. My friends have gone to the bar."

Brooke and Sebastian chose that moment to arrive.

"Sebastian." Holly inclined her head. She didn't know what was going on with the couple, and Brooke hadn't told her why they'd called things off, though her sister had cried buckets when she'd thought Holly wouldn't notice.

"Holly." Sebastian drew Brooke against his side in a silent statement. His steady gaze held a challenge.

Holly ran her finger around the rim of her glass and decided this was none of her business since Brooke was a big girl now. Holly shifted her gaze to the other man. "Sure, I'd love to dance."

"But she's dancing with me first," Angus said from behind her.

Holly jumped at the possessive hand that landed on her shoulder, her discomfort escaping a second time in a strained laugh.

"That true, O'Neil?" The man's gaze shifted to her.

"Holly?"

"You know my name?" Holly asked.

The weight of fingers disappeared, the hunky Angus distancing himself, but she could still sense the heat emanating from his big body until he stepped into her peripheral vision. Her contrary heart missed the physical contact, but his smell—something citrus with a hint of mint still filled her breaths. Not a combination she'd ever think of on her own, but it worked for her on every level.

"Sure, I'm Craig's friend."

"Oh." Boyfriend number three. *Rat bastard*. The liar who'd conveniently forgotten the fiancée he'd stashed in another town. That sealed it. "Thanks, but I did promise Angus the next dance." The heat at her back intensified as if he was watching her closely. *Danger, Holly Blackwood*.

Heck, an understatement.

Under this man's gaze, she felt like prey, mesmerized by the big and dangerous cat stalking her.

Holly shook herself from her fanciful thoughts. Her empty glass clinked on the tabletop. A fortifying breath later, she stood and sauntered the two steps to reach Angus. Without hesitation, she slid right into his personal space. Angus didn't blink. Instead, he wrapped his arm around her waist and guided her to the dance floor.

The frantic rock number came to a crashing crescendo just as they secured an empty spot, and the band segued into a soppy ballad about reunited lovers.

Holly swallowed, her gaze snapping to Angus. A smile curled his lips—one holding a silent question. He thought she'd refuse to slow dance with him. His dark brows rose, emphasizing his challenge.

The alcohol had made Holly brave. She sucked in a quick breath, stepped close, and pressed her breasts against his chest.

Big mistake.

Suddenly he swamped her senses, his citrus-mint aftershave, his size. He was several inches taller than her, bulkier, and he made her aware of her femininity. His black hair, tanned skin, and light blue eyes had attracted her attention when she'd answered the door tonight, and his smile, his scent, had won her favor. He was an attractive and fit man. Every one of her nerve endings twitched as his arms wrapped around her back and he held her with total confidence. Her stomach hollowed, and she lifted her head to steal a furtive gaze. His blue eyes blazed into hers, and his wink had her blushing. Even more mortifying, she was conscious of the dampness between her thighs, the silent goading of her body to take action.

She had to get control of herself. She couldn't let him know how he affected her.

No time for a man.

Stick to the netball plan.

After three exes, she'd concluded relationships weren't for her, and rugby playing boyfriends—forget it. She didn't need to put herself out there again to get her heart mauled like a rugby player at the bottom of a scrum.

This *thing* she felt whenever Angus looked at her, spoke with her, was nothing more than the alcohol talking. Yes, precisely the problem. Nerves had made her drink more than she should, a mistake since she'd eaten little dinner.

Men and women filled every inch of the dance floor now, not allowing for more than a shuffle. Most couples swayed on the spot, not bothering to move. Two smooching lovebirds hemmed them in place.

"Relax," he whispered, his breath warm against her cheek. "I won't bite."

Huh! That was the trouble. She wouldn't mind if he nibbled on her. In fact, her mind wasn't having any problem deciding on the exact places she'd like him to attack first.

Holly cleared her throat because she had to say something to break this sensual tension. Then she caught the gleam of his eyes, the way his attention drifted to her mouth, and every possible thought faded into oblivion.

"Unless you ask me to," he added in a husky voice.

"I don't want a man," she blurted.

"Oh?"

"No." Perhaps if she avoided his gaze, this dancing thing would go better. She burrowed against him but couldn't relax, not when every part of her quivered in recognition.

Heck, what was wrong with her? Hadn't experience

taught her anything? Those lessons her exes had dispensed had stuck—at least until she'd glimpsed Angus at close quarters tonight. For the first time, she'd coveted someone who belonged to her sister.

Angus cocked his head, interest gleaming in his blue eyes. "You mean you want nothing permanent, or you don't want sex at all? Or you get your sexual buzz from the female gender?"

She froze, the combination of warm breath across her earlobe and his amusement shocking the hell out of her. She'd picked dancing with him over Craig's friend. *Big, big mistake.*

"Not going to answer?" he taunted.

A ripple spread through her, and her breath hitched. Her mind slogged through murky waters, unable to function at pace.

Stupid alcohol.

And, if she stuck with the truth, it was *him* too. He did something to her—made her thoughts swirl and eddy and robbed her brain of oxygen. In the future, she'd keep away from Angus O'Neil. The man should come with danger signs.

The song ended—thankfully—and Angus released her. Seconds later, he captured her hand, twining their fingers together.

Shock reverberated through her, her gaze shot to his, and he grinned.

"You didn't think I'd let you go in the middle of our fascinating tête-à-tête?"

What conversation? He was doing the talking while she wanted to flee her thoughts. Yeah, time to go home. Past time. She'd leave the pub, catch the night bus home, and crawl into bed.

Alone.

He propelled her back to their table, shielding her from the shoves of other revelers, some of whom were taking celebrating a win to new inebriated levels.

"Good, you're back," Sebastian said. "Brooke and I are heading off now. You'll find your way home, yeah?"

Holly directed silent questions at her older sister. Was she okay with this? Brooke gave her a quick nod then winked, leaving Holly even more confused.

She started to demand answers and rethought her initial instincts. Brooke would tell her when she was ready. "Okay. Will you be home later?"

"Tomorrow morning," Brooke said in a soft voice.

Holly sighed. No coercion, then. She couldn't kick Sebastian's tight butt on her sister's behalf. Probably just as well. With her rotten luck, she'd break her toes and not be able to play netball for weeks. Okay, so no butt-kicking tonight.

"No problem, Brooke. I'll get a cab. See you tomorrow."

Thanks, her sister mouthed over her shoulder as she left with Sebastian.

"I apologize for Brooke's behavior," Holly said, feeling bad on Angus's behalf. This was not the right way to treat a date. "She's not usually this rude."

"It doesn't matter," Angus said. "We both knew there was no chemistry between us. With Brooke, it would be like fucking my sister."

Okaay. Holly reached for her drink. The faint tremor in her hand irked her. "That doesn't excuse her behavior or her lack of apology."

"You, on the other hand, interest me very much." His gaze locked onto hers, and she was left in no doubt of his intent.

"No, I don't require a man." Holly tilted her glass to her mouth and realized it was empty. Good grief. How had that happened?

"Don't you like sex?"

"I like sex," she snapped.

His brows arched upward in a silent question mark. "With men?"

"Yes, with a man." She had to answer that. Pride wouldn't let her lie.

"So, how will you have sex without a man? Wear out your vibrator?"

"I don't have one." *Oops*, her verbal filter was malfunctioning big time. "Not that it's any of your business."

"Don't you enjoy cuddling a man throughout the

night?"

"You're a cuddler?"

"Yes. I like sex, the feel and smell of a woman, and the way she cries out at the moment of climax. Don't you like the feel of a man powering into your body? The feel of his hands gliding over your skin? The taste of his cock in your mouth?"

Her mouth had dropped open, and she snapped it closed. "No."

Liar, liar, pants on fire. She not only enjoyed sex, but it always energized her, made her feel alive.

"I think you're lying."

"What are you? A mind reader?"

"Ah," he said with satisfaction. "You do like sex."

"I've already admitted it. Besides, is there something wrong with that? Still not seeing why I need a man. I have hands. They work well if I feel in the mood." Heat collected in her cheeks, and she was fiercely glad of the dimmer light near their table.

He reached for her hand and removed her wineglass. "You're going to break it if you're not careful."

She needed another drink. Yes, that would help, and she'd get this socializing thing going again. If Brooke quizzed her, she'd have names to lob back in her defense. Holly scanned their vicinity, searching for someone else to chat with. Everyone had paired up and swayed on the dance floor or propped up the bar. That left her with

Angus until she could escape.

"We could help each other," he suggested in a silky voice.

His implication rattled her so much she didn't pretend ignorance. "You don't know me."

"You love netball. You're dedicated and driven to succeed. That means dating and finding a man comes second. I'm attracted to you and, if you're honest with yourself, it's a mutual thing. We could help each other," he repeated, holding her gaze.

"But you could have any woman here," Holly said. "Why are you propositioning me?"

"You have a unique quality that suits me. You're ambitious and not interested in a permanent relationship. Am I wrong?"

Some of her tension faded. "No, you're right." Three mistakes were enough for a lifetime. It'd be a long spell until she'd trust a man again.

"Excellent. I'm offering a friends-with-benefits deal. I want sex with no strings. Friendship, honesty, and respect—yes. A wedding ring at the end—not so much."

"Friends-with-benefits?" A tiny voice inside her head screeched at her. Yes. Yes. *Yes.* "I don't know you. I met you tonight, which means we're nowhere near friends."

"We could be best friends. I like you already."

Yes! The tiny voice screamed again.

Holly took a quick breath. "I'm not that kind of girl."

2

YOU'RE NOT THE BOSS OF ME

HOLLY CHECKED HER WATCH and stood, her knees knocking until she braced enough to stand firm without wavering like a tree in a storm. *Bother, that last wine had been a mistake*.

"Thank you for your company tonight. And thanks for being so understanding about Brooke ditching you." *Not bad.* She sounded decisive and polite. Plus, she'd stayed for almost three hours.

Although the evening was still young, physical fatigue had her lagging. The music pounded through her head. The increasingly loud laughter and drunken shouts told her she was right to leave the party now.

Angus shot her a narrow-eyed glance. "Where are you going?"

"Home." Not quite the truth. She was running for cover

because this man scared away every scrap of her good sense. He made her think about sex—with him—when she needed to focus on her sport. Her future. Yeah, he alarmed her that much. His blunt proposition tempted her on so many levels. No, she was better to retreat—a strategic withdrawal before she lapsed into outright stupidity.

"I'll give you a lift."

"No, I'll catch a cab." She lied without blinking. "You stay and enjoy the party."

"Let me drive you home. There's no point in me staying if you're leaving." He shoved his beer away and stood. "Let's go."

"You're not the boss of me."

"I thought I'd be kind and save you the cab fare. Make sure you get home safely."

"Our apartment is out of your way." Holly fought the urge to grimace. This man was pushy. Not in a horrid, stalkerish way, though. He radiated determination—a man set on his course. Nothing she said would change his mind. Above the layers of alpha wolf, Angus O'Neil was a polite gentleman.

"You've had a few drinks, and I'd feel better if I knew you made it home." He gripped her arm and propelled her to the exit. "Please, it would help me to sleep better. Besides, I picked you and your sister up at your apartment. I would've driven you home, anyway."

Tension slid through Holly, a hint of self-preservation.

"I'd hate you to lose sleep over me." The man knew how to make his point.

"I won't if you let me escort you home."

"All right," she said with a heavy sigh of acceptance. She risked a glance at the man and caught the glint of humor in his eyes. Another sigh escaped as she broke the connection.

The ride home would take fifteen minutes tops, maybe less at this time of the night. She'd survive his company that long. It wasn't as if he could grope her while he was driving. She'd sit on her hands to avoid temptation from her side. *Yeah, that'd work.*

Angus guided her to his vehicle and opened the passenger door for her. He waited until she settled and closed it with a whoosh. This wasn't fair. She didn't want to like him, not when her three-man experience proved rugby players didn't good relationships make.

Angus climbed behind the wheel and backed out of the parking spot. Once he merged into the traffic, he cast a sidelong glance in her direction. "You didn't finish telling me about your training. You go running every morning. How many training sessions do you have each week?"

"I have team stuff most nights. Mostly it's drills and tactics, but sometimes we do promotional work."

"Do you enjoy the promo?"

"We've visited kids in the hospital and have traveled to several schools. I enjoy meeting the kids, especially if we get to play netball with them. That's always fun."

He halted for a red light. "I like the interaction with kids too. Passing on tips and doing a little coaching is rewarding. When I was seven, I remember the Canterbury players visiting my school. I already loved sports, but that's when I decided I wanted a rugby life."

Interest tugged at her despite her reservations. "What did your parents say?"

"They wanted me to go to university and study law, then join my father's practice."

"What did you do?"

"I went to university and studied law. But I also played rugby and still attended classes once I made the team. I finished my degree last year."

"Pleasing the parental units and doing what you wanted. Clever."

"Works for me. I focus on rugby now and will take up the law on my retirement. What about you?"

Holly let out a snort. "I'm doing a balancing act. Professional netballers don't receive as much money as rugby players. Not the junior ones, at any rate. I work part-time as a bank teller."

Something in her voice must have clued him in because he sent her a searching look as he paused at another light. "Problem?"

"I need to find another job, preferably one where the boss is more flexible. Either that or I need a second job to supplement my income." Heck. She pressed her lips together and glanced at her lap. Her verbal filter needed immediate replacement. She shouldn't blurt this private stuff to him.

Holly frowned out the window at the high-rise buildings and apartments, consternation filling her. Unease. She inhaled and immediately wished she hadn't when his citrus-mint fragrance filled her nostrils. Appalled at her instant physical response—a perking of her nipples—she focused on a group of boisterous pedestrians. Both male and female skipped along the sidewalk, shrieking with inebriated laughter.

"That's rough." His voice held sympathy. Understanding. "What will you do next?"

Holly jolted, and it took her a long moment to understand and direct her mind back to the conversation. "Sticking my head in the sand isn't working, so I'll have to hit the street and ask places if they have jobs."

"What about a job coaching netball?"

"The positions are volunteer. I need something that pays hard, cold cash." The McDonald's restaurant they passed was doing a brisk trade, and a new nightclub had a line of eager customers waiting to gain entrance.

"Rock and a hard place," he said.

"Yeah."

He pulled up outside her building at last. Holly reached to open the car door, but he placed his hand on her arm, stilling her. "Wait, I'll walk you to your apartment."

"You don't have to. This is a safe area." Damn, her pulse rate had changed up a gear just because he'd touched her. She was sick—doomed with a broken verbal filter and a faulty body that kept transmitting messages in conflict with her smarter brain.

"Humor me." He opened his door and jumped out, rounding his vehicle before she could offer another protest. "Besides, I wanted to ask you something."

"What?"

Instead of answering, he waited until she'd unfastened her seatbelt and grasped her hand. His palm abraded hers yet felt comfortable too. Perfect, in fact. *Too perfect.* She attempted to tug free, but he wouldn't let her.

He frowned, the streetlamp showing the furrow of his brow, the flash of irritation. "I thought we'd already established I don't bite. Promise I don't have cooties either."

She gave up the fight once she was standing on the pavement and was glad since she swayed. A surprised giggle escaped her, and he righted her in a straightforward move. "*Oops.* I think I drank too much."

"Which is why I wanted to walk you to your door," he said in a stern voice.

"You didn't want to kiss me goodnight?"

He barked out a laugh. "I've wanted to kiss you from the moment I saw you, but I won't follow my inclination. When I kiss you for the first time, we'll have clear heads and be on the same page. Our kiss will be something we both want."

"When you kiss me?"

"Count on it." He guided her through the unlocked door into the apartment building. "Shouldn't the door be locked?"

"The kids in the ground-floor apartment have heaps of friends visiting. They forget to lock it or leave the door open for their friends' entry. But we've had no problems."

"There's always the first occasion."

They climbed the stairs to the second floor. "You sound like Dad."

He tugged on her hand until Holly faced him. "No way do I feel like your father."

Holly took one look at his expression and gulped. Oh, boy.

No.

No, she wasn't considering his preposterous suggestion. Kisses with a man like Angus led to sex. Sex was never uncomplicated—not for her. Every time her emotions engaged, she ended up getting hurt.

"I'm not tempted," she said.

"Okay," he said. "What about if we became friends? No sex. Just friends who spend time together. Would that work for you?"

A *no* hovered on her lips as her brain overrode her body's expression of joy. But if she dated Angus, it would get

Brooke off her back, and even better, she wouldn't have to spend her free nights alone.

"Maybe." Her fuzzy mind searched for flaws in the agreement. "I'd have to think about it."

"Think how the situation could benefit us. We both have functions requiring a partner. If we attend together, we'll avoid messy complications or undue expectations from our dates."

"Your lawyer training is shining through," she said drily.

"Are my arguments working?"

"This is a ploy to put me off my guard."

His grin was a thing of beauty, a flash of humor that reverberated through his expression and lit his pretty eyes. "It's no secret I'd like more, but I can handle friendship. Of course, if you're worried you can't keep your hands to yourself..." He trailed off, the ringing taunt completing his sentence for him.

Right. That did it. *Game on.*

"I guess I could do friends. What happens if our schedules clash?"

His dark brows drew together. "I don't expect you to drop everything for me. I get you have commitments. We'll find a workable schedule." He moved closer and picked up a lock of her hair, rubbing it between finger and thumb.

Holly watched the slight movement, mesmerized by his strong fingers, his masculine hand. It was all too easy to imagine those digits roving her naked body. A spear of heat streaked through her, frisking every hot spot on the way to her feet.

"Goodnight, Angus." She forced the polite words and molded her lips to match the sentiment. "It was lovely meeting you."

That sexy gleam lit his blue eyes again. His pretty light blue eyes with lush dark lashes. Her breath caught as she realized her gaze was drifting and about to hit his mouth. *Dangerous territory.* She jerked it away to focus on the spy hole of her apartment door. His chuckle sent her spine poker-straight.

"I have your phone number," he said. "I'll call you."

"No, I—"

"Scared?"

"No." But it was a lie, and they both knew it.

HOLLY'S ALARM BURST INTO life, blaring out a recent pop hit at seven, an hour later than her normal weekday summons to rise. Groaning, she slapped at the clock, her hand meeting air until her brain engaged.

Oh, yeah.

Her belly ducked and dived as she swung her legs over the edge of her single bed and teetered to the far side of the room. She whacked the alarm twice. The silence was blissful.

Holly released a tiny groan. This was what happened when good sense gave way to her naughty, impish half.

A sharp twinge of protest careened pinball-like through her skull. Intent on escaping the screechy racket of body and mind, she meandered across the room, feet dragging in a tottering fashion.

She fell onto the bed with a grumble and rubbed her hands over her face. The temptation to crawl back between the sheets almost won, but from a cramped space at the back of her mind, she pulled out professionalism. If she wanted to make the team and advance to the national level, sacrifices were necessary.

The pep talk clawed through her headache and low-level nausea. Grimacing, she fumbled through the top drawer and pulled out a pair of leggings and a sports bra.

Twenty minutes later, after warm-up stretches, she left and turned toward Parnell and the Domain.

Sunday morning training runs were typically her favorite ones of the week. The traffic was lighter, and most people slept longer, leaving the sidewalks clear. This morning her hangover ruled, and not even the baking bread goodness drifting from a café lifted her mood. Each footfall ricocheted displeasure through her head and her aching muscles.

Holly inhaled, drawing the chilly morning air deep into her lungs. Once she reached the open expanse of green at the Doman and didn't need to worry about potholes or yappy dogs and their owners, she let her mind drift. It headed straight to Angus O'Neil.

Holly shoved the sexy man right back out and started on her routine of short sprints. She raced over the sports field, long strides taking her over a third of the area to a group of massive oak trees before she slowed to a jog.

She repeated the sequence until her lungs screamed, her brain whimpered, and sweat coated her limbs. The second she ceased her hard concentration, Angus leaped into prominence. *Again.*

Friends. *Bah.* She wasn't silly enough to think they'd keep to a platonic relationship. He was biding his time, waiting for her to crack. Well, newsflash. That wasn't gonna happen.

Holly ran two laps of the field, checked her watch, and headed back to the apartment. She had time for a shower and a light breakfast before she left for training. The coach was announcing the team for Wednesday's game today, and she didn't intend to give Robyn Marshall a reason not to read out her name.

AT A LOOSE END on Wednesday evening, since his cousin Connor had backed out of their plans, Angus decided to watch the Blue Dynamos game in person. He parked his vehicle and wove through the clusters of people ambling toward the stadium. The scent of cooking meat and coffee floated in the air, coming from food trucks parked near the entrance.

He'd wanted to ring Holly ever since he'd left her on Saturday night, but he'd known she was uneasy with his attention and wanted to backpedal. His instincts had never steered him wrong with women. He'd intrigued her, and he needed to give her time.

But not too long.

She'd captivated him, and he'd thought of her at odd times of the day. Watching her play netball was a non-confrontational way of taking the next step in their little game.

Men and women of all ages and sizes packed the stadium on the North Shore, most dressed in the navy and white team colors. Aftershave and perfume battled with a hint of hamburgers. The distinct sharpness of disinfectant drifted from a cleaner's bucket as she mopped up a spill.

Conversation ebbed and flowed as attendees located their seats and their friends. Background music, something with a peppy beat, added to the cacophony. Although Angus had known netball was popular in Australasia, he hadn't expected the Wednesday night sell-out crowd.

Angus squeezed past a family of three teenage girls, their mother, and grandmother—at a guess. He'd thought about watching the game on television, but he'd wanted to see Holly in person. He dropped into his seat beside the woman he'd decided was the grandmother.

The gray-haired, bespectacled woman sent him a friendly grin. "Angus O'Neil, isn't it?"

"Yes." His reply emerged guarded. He wanted to watch and plan, not engage in polite chitchat.

"Have you come to watch someone in particular?" The woman's voice held a smidgeon of coy along with the nosiness.

"One of my friends is on the team. I don't get a chance to watch her play very often."

"I suppose you spend a lot of time away from home with your rugby commitments."

"Yes." Aware of his public persona and the lectures drummed into the team by management, Angus bit back his impatience.

The speaker system burst into life with the beginning notes of a current top-forty hit. A cheer lifted the roof, the exuberance echoing through the indoor stadium. Everyone in the audience thumped the sponsors' thunder sticks together in a rowdy *bang, bang, bang.* The players of the two teams appeared on the court, taking an end each to commence their warm-up. Each player ran through sprints, jumps, and ball skills. The limbering up routine was as familiar to him as the game.

"The Dynamos are playing well," the woman said. "My name is Marge, by the way."

"Nice to meet you, Marge." Angus spied Holly running onto the court. His gaze fastened on her long legs displayed enticingly beneath the short navy blue and white uniform dress. She'd pulled back her honey-blonde hair in a tight braid, and her face bore concentration. An Amazon preparing for battle came to mind.

The music halted, and a male voice ran through the names of the teams and their on-court positions. Cheers accompanied his announcement, and anticipation surged within Angus. Holly had made the team, and he thrilled at the thought of seeing her in action.

Players took their positions on the court. The center for the Dynamos stood in the center circle, and the umpire blew her whistle. The battle began.

The ball flew the length of the court, thrown from player to player. Crisp, clean passes made the play appear effortless, but Angus understood how much training went into ensuring the ball traveled fluidly to the goal circle.

The goal shoot aimed. The keeper timed her jump and leaped, her arms outstretched in her efforts to put off the goalie. The ball sailed smoothly through the net.

Goal.

The umpire blew her whistle, and everyone ran back into position to the roar of the crowd and the din of thunder sticks.

Angus cheered with everyone else and leaned forward in his seat, eager to see Holly play once the opposition took their center pass. She was the goal keep this week. His gaze trailed her, taking in her intent focus. Determination etched on her face, her jaw tight, eyes watchful, while her body—all coiled spring and power—backed up the attitude.

The opposition passed the ball back and forth from player to player, more cautious than the Dynamos. Their uncertainty gave the defense players time to read the play and anticipate the opposition's next move. Holly darted from the circle, jumping high, her fingers tipping the ball. The crowd roared, then groaned in sympathy when the opposition gathered up the loose pass.

"Is that your friend?" Marge asked.

"Yes."

"She's pretty."

"Yes, she is." If he had his way, their acquaintance would bloom into something more.

The first fifteen-minute quarter flew by, the Dynamos clinging to a slender three-goal lead. It was an intense game, the lead seesawing between the two teams until the very end.

With two minutes on the clock, Angus, along with the rest of the crowd, was on his feet and chanting encouragement. Long blue thunder sticks pounded together in an ear-splitting racket. Even the players were having difficulty hearing the umpire's whistle to halt play.

"Go, Holly," he whispered as the ball headed in her

direction. "Now is the time for an intercept."

She focused on the ball, her game-face tacked into place. She'd hear nothing except the thud of her heart, the cheers of the crowd, the screams from their reserve bench blending into white noise.

The opposition was having trouble feeding the ball into the circle, both Holly and the Dynamo goal defense making progress difficult. The two women were everywhere, marking their opposites and jumping to distract play. The opposition threw and bounce-passed the ball around the goal circle, trying to find an opening. The wing attack caught the ball, saw the signal from the goal shoot. Up, up, up the lob went, and Angus saw Holly eye it the entire time. She jumped at the same time as the opposition, both grabbing the ball. After a brief skirmish, Holly gained possession.

Angus held his breath, waiting for the umpire to blow her whistle for illegal contact. It didn't happen. Off-footed, the opposition was slow to regroup, and the ball flew to the Dynamo's end of the court in four quick passes. The Dynamo goal attack claimed the ball. It was near the goalpost, and she shot. The ball circled the rim, wobbled, then fell through the net.

"Goal to the Dynamos!" the announcer cried over the loudspeaker.

The crowd roared, the thunder sticks even louder than earlier.

Angus took his seat and studied play. That goal broke the opposition team, and the players offered little challenge to the next center pass. The ball zapped from player to player without a hitch until it arrived at the goal circle. Aware of the ticking clock, the goal attack shot from far out. The ball bounced off the goal rim.

A groan filled the stadium.

The shooter and the two defense players jostled for possession.

The umpire's whistle blew. "Contact!"

The goal keep stood next to the shooter, not allowed to contest the ball. The shooter aimed. Missed. Another tussle for the ball ensued. This time the shooter snatched it first. She shot, and the ball dropped through the net. The whistle signaled a legal goal.

Angus glanced at the clock. Mere seconds left. No way to lose now. Almost as the thought formed, the hooter signaled the end of the game.

On his feet, Angus applauded. Fans erupted in shrill whistles and cheers, and the din of the audience and thunder sticks filled the stadium.

A win to Holly's team by two goals.

Angus dropped into his seat, relief beating a tattoo through his veins. It was a damn sight harder watching a close-fought match than experiencing it as a team member.

Marge tapped him on the shoulder. "Your girl played

well."

"Yes, she did." With form like that, she'd make the starting lineup for the next game. She should feel confident with her performance.

Television reporters interviewed the winning and losing captains while players signed autographs for fans. Angus stared at Holly, tamping down his desire to sprint over to the court and lay one on her—a reward for a game well played.

Now wasn't the time.

Something of his thoughts seeped into his expression because Marge flicked her hand in dismissal. "Go and see your girl. They'll recognize you and let you through."

Angus nodded, not wasting his energy to argue and tell Marge they were merely friends. "I'll wait a bit longer. Holly will need to warm down first."

"It was nice to meet you, Angus. Good luck with your game next weekend."

"Thanks, Marge."

Her wrinkled face softened, and she moved in, surprising him with a swift hug. "I don't get to many games. The best I can do is watch you on TV and cheer out my heart. Maybe I'll see you in the ladies' magazines."

Angus snorted. "You shouldn't believe anything you read in those."

Marge patted his shoulder, humor twinkling in her eyes, then left with her family. The stadium emptied of people while the players proceeded through their stretching routine.

Angus hesitated—uncharacteristic for him—while he decided how to approach Holly. He wanted to plunge into an intimate relationship with her, and holding back was chafing.

No pressure, he reminded himself. Yeah, he could do casual. Hell, he had to, or he'd frighten her off, but the truth was she intrigued him on so many levels. For the first time since the failure of his marriage, a woman had got under his skin.

A burst of humor rose to the surface. Treat her like a fish on a line. *Gently, gently,* or she'd evade capture. *Capture. Hell, just call me Angus the Barbarian.*

Aware he was the last person left in his row, he stood and made his way toward courtside. He waited until Holly jogged past and called out to her.

"Holly, you want a lift home?" Since this was a home game, the team members would have traveled to the stadium individually instead of arriving on a bus.

She halted and stared at him in dismay. "Angus? What are you doing here?"

"I came to see you play." He watched the quick expressions chase over her face—surprise, pleasure, chagrin, and wariness—and wanted to smile. While he mightn't have spoken to her since Saturday night, she'd thought about him.

Today was an excellent day.

"So, would you like a lift home? Have a quick meal first?"

Color flushed her cheeks after the exertion of the game, and damp wisps of hair had escaped her tight braid to frame her face. She looked gorgeous, and he had to stop himself from doing a quick visual scan of her torso and legs and pissing her off in the process.

"I am starving," she said. "I'm always too nervous to eat before the game."

"Where should I meet you?"

She shifted her weight, hesitated, then rushed into speech. "By the players' door. It's by the admin office on the opposite side of the stadium to the public entrance. I'll be half an hour yet because I need to grab a quick shower. Are you sure you want to wait?"

"No problem. I have my e-reader to keep me entertained."

Her mouth dropped open as she stared.

"What's the matter? Last time I checked, I only had one head, and all my features are in the right place."

"You read?"

Angus chuckled. "We have a lot of spare hours while we're traveling to and from games. I like to read or listen to audiobooks. What do you do to fill in the time?"

"Sleep and read romances." A trace of defiance emanated from her as if she expected him to make a wisecrack about her reading material.

"I've read a romance or two in my time," he replied. "You know my vehicle. I'll see you in about half an hour."

It was closer to three-quarters of an hour later before Holly slid into the passenger seat.

"Sorry, some of the girls take ages in the shower."

"You should have told them you had a hot man waiting for you. They might have taken pity on you."

"They had enough nosy questions without me adding fuel to the fire," she said, her tone sharp. Then, as if she regretted her outburst, she jerked her head at his e-reader. "What are you reading?"

"A book about the history of food. Normally I read fiction, but I like cooking, and this one appealed to me. It's interesting, and the author has a dry wit."

"What do you cook?"

The relaxed conversation went some way to settling Angus and the rush of unusual nerves stalking his belly. "I try everything. Most of the time, my dishes turn out okay, but I have a few disasters. I like pasta and curries. During the rugby season, I use the crockpot to save time. Do you cook?"

"Mum taught Brooke and me to cook, but I don't do a lot these days. Brooke worries about her weight, so we eat salad and salmon or something low in calories."

"There's a great fish place near my apartment."

Holly chewed her bottom lip. He caught the tormenting

action with his glance, and his reaction to it plunged the length of his body.

"Is it expensive?" she asked. "I don't have much money with me."

"No problem. How about if I whip up a quick pasta dish at my place?"

Relief flitted through her, followed by quick wariness.

"Do you need to ring your sister to let her know you're with me?" He dug deep for a calm tone. There was no way on earth he'd ever hurt her or any other woman, but she didn't know his character. Not yet.

"Yeah, I'll give her a quick call and let her know when I'll be home."

Angus pushed aside his slight indignation and drove toward the city and over the bridge spanning the harbor. Lights twinkled from windows and streetlamps, making the CBD sparkle like a woman wearing a rhinestone gown.

"Did you enjoy the game?" she asked, breaking the silence that had fallen between them.

"I did. At the start of the fourth quarter, I thought the other team might've had the game in the bag. Did your coach give you guys a rev?"

"You could say that," Holly said drily. "Her tongue is like a sword when she dissects player performance. I'm frightened of her."

Angus grinned because he'd had a coach or two over the years who'd inspired a healthy fear. "Her tirade did the trick. Your team was on fire. You played well, Holly. I think it's safe to say you've secured your place in the team for the next game."

"Do you think so?"

Angus pulled up at a traffic light and tossed her a smile. "I do."

"Do you have a home game next week?"

"No, we're playing in Melbourne. We fly out on Friday morning." He wanted to tease her and ask if she'd miss him. Only biting his tongue kept the smartass quip unspoken. The last thing he wanted was to scare her or appear too intense. She hovered like a wary animal as it was, and if he misjudged his next move, she'd flee.

3

GARLIC AND PESTO WITH A SIDE OF ANGUS

ANGUS HAD MADE A special trip to watch her play netball. Holly turned the fact over in her mind, searching for meaning, for subtext. She slid a glance toward Angus, his big hands competent on the wheel as he wove around an illegally parked car and the boisterous and shouting passengers who'd tumbled from vehicles to high-five friends.

Of course, her team members, with their dirty minds, had read the implications and added facts together like champion math prodigies. The power of their raunchy suggestions still had her squirming and uncomfortable, her cheeks flaming in the darkness.

"We're just friends," she'd said, or at least tried to tell

them.

The girls' hoots of disbelief had resounded through the changing rooms. She gulped at the memory and was thankful for the dim vehicle interior.

She'd stop reading spicy romances and nip this unhealthy tendency before her erotic thoughts became a habit.

A tiny snort emerged, tinged with panic and self-ridicule.

"Something wrong?" Angus asked.

"No, of course not," she said hurriedly and bit her lip to still any other telltale sounds.

Last night, the bad-boy pirate in her latest read had morphed into dark-haired Angus, right down to his cocky smile. She'd stepped into the heroine's tightly laced dress and kept with historical fact. No panties to shield her aching flesh. Result: instant hot, instant bothered.

She'd tossed and turned, as restless as a frigate riding the ocean swells, and given into the inevitable, running her fingers over her swollen pussy, strumming her clit, and driving herself to a heart-rattling climax. At the same time, pirate Angus did naughty things to her weak and willing body.

All that after one meeting.

This second meeting was gonna play hell with tonight's sleep patterns.

"Aren't you talking to me?"

"Ah, sorry. My next game. Um, we have one more home game, one in Invercargill, and the next after that in Brisbane," she said, answering his question with only the barest quiver in her voice to give away her attack of nerves.

"How's the job hunting going?"

She flinched. "The bank manager told me today she needs a full-time teller. A clear warning salvo. If I don't increase my hours, I'll lose my job."

"I thought the bank was one of your main sponsors," Angus said, a trace of surprise in his husky voice.

"I work for the opposition."

"Why don't you approach your sponsor bank? Surely they'd like the idea of a franchise netball player working for them."

She gaped at him while mentally slapping her face. "Wow! I should've thought of that myself. I was thinking about a waitressing job or pub or bike courier work."

"Approaching the opposition is worth a shot." Angus pulled into a parking building beneath a waterside apartment complex. "You should try their head office first. They'll know if there are branch vacancies that might suit your hours."

Holly followed Angus into his apartment, her gaze going straight to the enormous picture window that showcased the twinkling lights around the harbor. During the day, he'd see yachts and ferries and maybe some of the cruise ships that berthed at Princes Wharf.

Ripping her gaze off the view, she scanned the ample open space of the kitchen and living areas—the granite counters, the gleaming appliances, and the squishy black leather two-seaters that delineated the living area. Red and white accents livened up the midnight black and stopped the room from slipping into gloomy. A bold red-and-black rug in geometric patterns cushioned her feet as she trailed Angus.

Two words summed up the decor. Designer chic. She hated to think how much the rental was per month. Way out of her price range, that was for sure.

"Come and talk to me while I'm cooking," Angus said. "Would you like wine?"

"Just one glass," Holly said. "I'll give Brooke a call first."

Angus sent her a teasing smile. "Did you have a headache on Sunday?"

"Yes, smartarse. What sort of pasta are we having?" She plucked her phone from her bag and hit speed dial. Brooke didn't answer, so she left a quick message before turning back to Angus.

"I thought I'd keep it simple. How does spaghetti with pesto and garlic bread sound?"

"Perfect," she said, her stomach giving a happy rumble at the thought of imminent food. And better, since there was garlic involved, he wouldn't even consider kissing her. High fives all 'round.

"There's a bottle of Marlborough sav in the fridge door.

Glasses are in the cupboard to your right. Pour one for me too."

"Sure." Holly was glad of a task to occupy herself because watching Angus stretch and bend to grab the items he required from different cupboards was doing her head. The way the denim stretched across his butt. *Yum.*

Her hand trembled as she reached into the cupboard for wineglasses. She clenched and unclenched her fingers, reassured when her hand became rock steady. Just a casual dinner, she reminded herself. With garlic. Yeah, she had her friend fence firmly erected. Nothing would go wrong.

Half an hour later, perspiration beaded her brow and brought a clammy sensation to her back. Every breath she took was full of garlic and pesto with a side of Angus. She couldn't identify his brand of aftershave, but it'd become her favorite. She'd never inhale that citrus-mint again without thinking of him and her craving for hot and heavy sex.

"Grub's up," Angus said, handing her a plate of spaghetti.

Like a zombie, she shuffled over to the small table she'd set at his request, her mind fogged with thoughts inappropriate for the occasion.

"I'm not sure if friendship will work between us." The words shot from her mouth before seeking permission from her brain. She plonked onto a chair, astounded—no—irked at her loquaciousness. Now he'd ask questions and expect answers.

"Why?" He joined her at the table and tipped his head to the side, a tiny grin playing around his lips.

Sexy lips. Kissable lips. They'd had a starring role in her midnight fantasies.

"Holly." Amusement filled his voice and pulled Holly from her momentary lapse. The wretched man was laughing at her.

"Because I keep having inappropriate thoughts about you," she said with acute frustration.

"I noticed you ogling my butt."

She swallowed once, and heat surged to her cheeks. Bother the man. "You're not helpful to my mental health."

Instead of tossing a smartarse comment at her, he said, "Eat your dinner while it's hot. Would you like garlic bread?"

"Yes, please. It's one of my favorites, but I don't get to eat it often."

"Because of Brooke and her diet?"

"Yes."

She helped herself to a piece and took a healthy bite. Butter and garlic oozed across her taste buds, and she let out a blissful moan of pleasure. She closed her eyes to savor the flavors better and chewed. Her eyes popped open, and she discovered him watching her. Lust glinted in his blue eyes.

"I'm not squeezing you into a friend box either. It was

pleasure and hell watching you dash around the netball court all long legs and concentration."

"I told you this wouldn't work," she said with regret. She liked him already and enjoyed his company. She'd do it tough going back to her pre-Angus world.

He twirled spaghetti around his fork before meeting her gaze. "There's no reason we can't change the boundaries we'd agreed on earlier."

The heat in his blue eyes made it difficult for her to concentrate on her dinner. She wanted to wrench her gaze away from his, but she was weak. Her throat worked in a hard swallow. "I have to focus on my netball, otherwise I'll waste the sacrifices I've made so far. My goal is to make the national team to play Australia, and fingers crossed, the Commonwealth Games squad the year after."

Back when she was a five-year-old, and her mother was dying from cancer, she'd promised she'd try. And now, she liked to think her mother was proud of her accomplishments.

"My rugby is important to me. That's why the two of us together are perfect. We both understand the sacrifices necessary to climb to the top. There won't be any bitching because we never see each other or miss a birthday if we're away or have training. We're aware our sport takes precedence."

Holly shoved spaghetti in her mouth to stop herself from shouting, *Hell, yes. Let's do it.*

No, sex with Angus was a terrible notion, but the thought of seeing him with another woman cut like a rusty knife. Still not ready to talk, she reached for her slice of garlic bread. *Botheration.* Platonic friends was a challenge—he was too tempting—which made him right. Friends-with-benefits was the obvious solution.

She swallowed a mouthful of garlic bread and grabbed her wine. *I'll thank him and tell him no.*

"All right," she said and clapped a hand to her mouth in horror. "Angus, this is a terrible idea."

His blue eyes darkened. "It's one of my better suggestions."

"A trial basis," she said, backtracking rapidly. "If our...ah...thing interferes with my netball, I reserve the right to call it off."

"That is a given." Angus picked up his glass and lifted it in a toast. "To friendship and excellent sex."

Holly felt an unwilling grin tugging at her lips. "To friendship." She paused. *Heck, who was she kidding? She'd been doomed from the moment he'd said hello when he'd picked her and Brooke up for the party.* "And outstanding sex."

The minute she'd made a verbal agreement, the tension in her eased, and she knew this was the right thing to do. Rejection would land her in Stress City because she'd worry about what might have been—the alternatives. At least this way...

"How do you like the pasta?"

"Delicious," she said. "The garlic bread is tasty too."

He picked up the plate of bread. "Have another piece. I want to hear your sexy little moan when you take a bite. It did all sorts of interesting things to my dick."

"Thanks for sharing," she said, restraining her grin with difficulty. She enjoyed his bluntness, and her return lobs didn't seem a deterrent. Maybe a kaput verbal filter was an advantageous thing. She accepted another slice of bread and bit into the buttery, garlicky goodness.

"It's refreshing seeing a woman enjoy her food. Finicky eaters irritate me. This diet or that diet when they're already so skinny their hips are like sharp knives."

"I like to eat." Fatigue hit Holly suddenly, and a yawn burst free. "Sorry."

Angus chuckled. "No problem. Finish your dinner, and I'll take you home."

Her gaze shot to his. Didn't he want to—

"Yes, I want to fuck you," he said, following her thoughts without difficulty. "But you're exhausted after your game. If you fall asleep in the middle of sex, it will hurt my ego. I might never recover. I can wait."

"I don't know if I can."

Angus snickered. "Waiting won't kill you."

Half an hour later, he drove her home. He pulled up outside her apartment and turned to her. "Thanks for dinner. I enjoyed it."

"You did all the work. I reaped the reward."

"But you're going to give me a kiss to even the slate." He clicked his seatbelt free and leaned over.

Her hand crept up to her mouth. "I have garlic breath," she mumbled, wishing she'd reconsidered her earlier plan.

"Don't care," he said. "No vampire blood in me. I can handle a little garlic."

He'd eaten garlic bread too, she remembered, although not as much as her.

He cupped her face between his hands and pressed their foreheads together. "Just one kiss," he said. "Give me the reality to conjure up while I'm alone in my apartment."

Before she could speculate about precisely what he meant, his lips met hers. It was a gentle getting-to-know-you type of kiss, but it soon morphed into hello-gorgeous-let-me-lay-one-on-you.

After her initial hesitation, she forgot about garlic breath and opened to him. His tongue stroked hers, and he playfully nibbled on her bottom lip. She gasped as desire hooked her, drawing her under until her world consisted solely of him and the sensations he sent soaring through her body.

When he drew back, their breaths were harsh and choppy.

"I knew we'd create magic between us," he said. "Think how it will feel when we're naked."

A shudder worked down her spine, hot X-rated

thoughts zipping through her like a seesawing game of netball. And she'd hoped her decision to have a relationship with Angus would help her sleep.

Foolish woman.

"Do you have your cell phone?"

"Yes, although I don't use it very much." Another cost-cutting exercise.

"Give it to me," he ordered.

Shrugging, she burrowed in the side pocket of her gear bag and handed him her phone. He programmed in his number.

"I'll call you," he said. "Our schedules might not mesh, but we can still get our sexting on."

"Huh?" Holly's brows shot upward, and she didn't have to pretend confusion.

He grinned, his teeth a white flash in the streetlamp's illumination. "If we can't meet in person, a little phone sex will help knock the edge off any residual tension."

"Oh, I haven't tried that before."

"Nothing for you to worry about, my virgin sexter. You go with what feels good." With that, he kissed her cheek, gave her a grin that charmed her to the tips of her striped red-and-white sock-clad toes.

"Thanks for dinner and the lift home." Holly grabbed her bag and unfolded from the car. The bumps and bruises she'd collected during the game protested, and she winced.

"Got some arnica rub?" he asked, missing nothing. "It

helps me."

"I use it too. Netball is a non-contact sport, but the games are physical. The goal shooter tonight owned a pair of nasty, pointy elbows, and she used them on my ribs at every opportunity."

Angus's chuckle sent her on her way, happiness putting a spring in her step despite myriad aches and pains.

Bad idea or not—that remained to be seen—she had herself a friendly fuck buddy. Perhaps her luck was making a U-turn.

HER CELL PHONE RANG half an hour after Angus dropped her off. Holly tightened the lid on the tub of arnica and answered absently, expecting Brooke. She'd only seen her sister in passing since Saturday night. "Hey, Brooke. Are you staying with Sebastian again?"

"It's Angus." The husky voice sent instant messages of lust zipping through her. He'd mentioned phone sex... A shiver frisked every pleasure point as it slipped over her skin.

"Hi." Her voice emerged on a croak, and she coughed to clear her throat. "Did you want something?"

"Right now, I wish I hadn't left you. What are you wearing?"

She glanced down at her naked body. "Granny pants and

a pair of old flannelette pajamas. They have blue-and-white checks."

"I've just had a shower. I touched myself and thought of you."

Her heart flip-flopped as her mind conjured up the image—water pouring over his body, the soap perfume filling the air, and steam fogging the shower cubicle. Her mind wandered to his strong fingers, curled around his shaft, the slow pump of his hand as he masturbated. Heat rushed through her cheeks, and she flapped her hand to cool her face.

"Did you hear what I said?"

"Yes. Um, you did?"

"I haven't come yet." His voice seduced her clear across Auckland.

"I'm naked," she blurted.

"Are you now? What color are your nipples?"

She glanced at her breasts. "Pale pink."

"Nice," he whispered.

Holly swallowed and gave in to her naughty urges. She trailed her fingers across the curve of her breast and brushed one nipple. It pulled tight while she watched.

"What are you doing?"

"Touching my nipple."

"Did it go hard?"

"Yes."

A harsh breath whistled down the line. "Are you in your

bedroom?"

"Yes, I was rubbing arnica on my bruises. They look like a patchwork quilt covering my body."

"Are they sore?"

"A little tender. I've had worse."

"If I were there, I'd rub the arnica on for you. Then I'd wash my hands with soap, so there's no residue, and I'd love you with my mouth and fingers."

"No preliminaries?"

"After I finished treating your bruises, you'd feel very relaxed. Lie flat on the bed and spread your legs."

"Now?"

"Now," he confirmed, his tone almost stern. "Put your phone on speaker. Tell me when you're ready."

Holly hesitated for long seconds, then pressed the speaker button on her phone and swung her legs onto her single bed. She leaned back against her pillows and parted her thighs. "I'm ready."

"Good girl."

Holly closed her eyes, focusing on his husky voice.

"Open your eyes," he directed. "Whenever we're together, I want to watch your responses. It helps me gauge what to do next."

"Sounds as if you have lots of experience." Her voice came out sharper than she'd intended.

"I'm older than you. Holly, I'm not going to make excuses. I've been with other women, but I won't have sex with anyone else as long as our agreement exists. You have my word. All right? Holly?"

"Okay." If he broke his word, she'd string him up by the balls.

"Part your legs as wide as you can. Have you done that?"

She followed his instruction and cool air brushed her hot flesh, making her ultra-aware of the thrum of her pulse and the tick of her alarm clock. "Yes."

"Yes, Angus."

"Yes, Angus," she repeated as if under a spell.

"Now, take your right forefinger and trace your mouth. Pretend the finger is mine, and I'm staring into your eyes."

Her hand rose to her lips before he'd finished speaking. Her eyes squeezed shut as her finger caressed her bottom lip.

"Eyes open," Angus barked.

Her eyes flicked open, guilt making her lips purse. "Yes, Angus." How the devil had he known she'd shut her eyes? Her gaze slid to her curtains, which were firmly shut against the night. Not that anyone could peer through the windows since their apartment was on the second floor.

"Dip your finger into your mouth and moisten it to the knuckle. Then I want you to circle your areola. Do it slowly and tell me how you feel. Describe how your nipple is responding to your touch."

"Yes, Angus." She licked her finger, and a corresponding tug jerked between her legs. How could such an innocent touch feel so damn exciting?

"I'm waiting, Holly."

"When I licked my finger, I felt it all over my body. I can feel the cool air on my pussy." Her finger drifted over her nipple, a delicate touch but a powerful one. She repeated the move. "It feels wonderful."

"Are you wet?"

"Yes, Angus." That had happened the moment she'd heard his husky voice.

"Take your nipple between your finger and thumb and twist it hard, to a point shy of pain, then with your other hand skim your fingers along your folds. Don't touch your clit. Just use enough pressure to tease yourself."

Her pinch of fingers telegraphed a rapid message to her sex, and moisture greeted her questing finger. A jolt shot through her. "I'm going to touch my clit."

"No, not yet," he said. "This is what I want you to do. Lift your finger to your mouth and lick it clean. Taste your arousal."

Holly found her finger at her lips even before the thought firmed in her brain. There was something about his voice—the husky note of command—that had her acting without hesitation.

"Tell me how it tastes, Holly." Silent authority rippled through his words.

"It tastes...a bit hard to describe. Fresh. A bit musky too."

"Good girl," he said. "Now, I want you to climb into bed and go to sleep."

"But—"

"You have objections to anticipation?" His lazy humor carried down the line, a man who was sure of himself.

"You won't know if I get myself off," she retorted.

"Yes. I will. I have an inbuilt radar for bullshit."

A snort escaped her. "You're all talk."

"Why don't you try it and see?"

"I will."

He laughed. "See you tomorrow. Dream of me, beautiful." Angus ended the call with an abrupt click.

She stared at her phone in disbelief. Her entire body vibrated with need, cried out for petting. Unbidden, her hand trailed over her hip and came to a rest at the line of pubic hair. Her clit pulsed, a silent urge to give in to her sexual impulse. Instead, she curled her fingers and gave a soft groan, then she muttered under her breath.

She wasn't sure what sort of game Angus played, but *she* decided how the ending went.

Her fingers cruised over her clit. Once. Twice. On the third stroke, she tumbled into climax, her pussy clenching on emptiness. Disgusted with herself for playing Angus's sexual games, she plumped her pillow and shoved the irritating man aside.

"Take that, Angus O'Neil."

ANGUS STARED AT HIS erection. "Fuck," he muttered.

He'd wanted to hear her husky voice. That's all. Instead, he'd let impulse take over, and he'd plunged into sexy with an edge of kink. His ex-wife's voice popped into his head. *"You need therapy. You're weird and unnatural. No woman likes that kind of stuff."*

He stalked to his en suite, the tiles cool beneath his bare feet, and turned on the shower. The cold water pounding against his chest made him wince, but by the time he'd run through several rugby training drills in his head, the frigid shower had done the trick. The citrus shower gel had cleared his head, and the tinge of regret had fled. After roughly toweling off the worst of the water, he slid between the sheets and willed himself to sleep.

This was a casual relationship designed to please two busy people who didn't have time or the inclination to pursue a permanent one. Yeah. A little vanilla sex would take off the edge and relax him. He'd be too busy to worry about anything else.

"HOLLY, WAKE UP."

Feeling as if she needed another four hours of sleep,

Holly groped for the bedside lamp and blinked enough to focus on her sister. "Brooke? What is it? What's the time?"

"It's six. Almost time for your alarm to go off, anyway," her sister said, waving her arms. Today's sophisticated perfume with its notes of amber and the Orient invaded the room.

Holly pushed up on her elbow, remembered she was nude, and grabbed the sheet to screen her breasts.

Brooke's brows rose. "Did you have someone sleep over? And where did you get that bruise?"

"You woke me to give me a hard time?" Holly didn't bother to hide the edge of her temper. "I haven't seen you since Saturday night after you disappeared with Sebastian. What's going on with you?"

A burst of excitement flashed across her sister's face. A wide grin followed, and she waggled her left hand in front of Holly's nose. "Sebastian and I got married. We're leaving on our honeymoon later today."

"Honeymoon," Holly parroted, her brain lagging steps behind. Brooke was married? "But you told me you and Sebastian had broken up. What's changed?"

"He told me he couldn't live without me. We talked a lot and hashed out our problems. I've been miserable without him, Holly. I know you don't understand, but I'm hoping you'll be happy for me."

"Let me get dressed, and you can tell me all about it."

"Sebastian is picking me up at nine. We're going to drop

by to see Mum and Dad before we head to the airport."

"Airport? Where is this honeymoon taking place?"

"We're spending a week at the Aggie Gray resort in Western Samoa."

"Nice," Holly said, a spurt of envy bringing discomfort. This was Brooke's honeymoon. She deserved a week of relaxation in the sun.

"I'll put on the coffee while you dress." Brooke sashayed out of the bedroom and broke out into song in the kitchen. A toast and a coffee aroma soon wafted in the air.

Holly jumped out of bed and grabbed the running gear she'd set out the previous night. It paid to be organized because her brain often required a kick start. A few minutes later, she strode into the kitchen, feeling more alert.

"Have you told Mum and Dad?"

"I rang them last night. I tried to ring you, but you weren't at home. Training again?"

"No, we had a game."

"Ah, that accounts for the bruising. I hope you used your elbows for a few return shots on the opposition."

Holly rolled her eyes. "We're talking about you, not about netball."

"Yes, Mum and Dad know."

"How did they take it?" Holly knew their mother didn't think Sebastian was good for Brooke. Brooke's mother—Holly's stepmother—since Brooke's mother and their father had been high school sweethearts. An argument had broken them up, and the surprise pregnancy remained that way for a long time—until after Holly's mother had died of cancer.

Brooke's smile faltered. "They'll get used to it soon. They'll have to. Sebastian isn't going anywhere."

Holly softened. "Are you happy?"

"Insanely," Brooke said.

Holly accepted the mug of coffee Brooke handed her and took a quick sip. "That's great. I'm pleased for both of you."

"I knew you would be. Are you going for your usual run?"

"Yeah." Holly drank another mouthful and set the mug aside. "I'd better not drink anymore, or I'll end up with the stitch."

"I need to pack, so I'll get started. I take it you'll want to stay here at the apartment."

"What?"

"Sebastian's apartment is bigger than this one. It makes sense for me to move rather than Sebastian. I've sorted out the rent, and it's paid up until the end of the month."

"Oh." Dumbfounded, Holly sought the right thing to say. *Stupid.* Of course, a married couple wanted to move in together. "Sure. No problem. I'd better get going, or I'll be late for work. The boss lady will sack me if I give her a chance." Bending her head, she concentrated on her shoes and tying the laces.

"Tara was a bitch at school, and she hasn't changed much," Brooke said. "I'll make you something for breakfast."

"Thanks, but I can grab an apple. Have fun on your honeymoon." She forced a cheerful smile in Brooke's direction and waved a farewell, steering her flood of emotions—fear, apprehension, a healthy dose of panic—on a straight course until she shut the front door behind her. Alone, her grip on her turmoil wobbled.

Crap. What the hell was she going to do now?

Outside, the early morning air slapped her cheeks and cleared her mind. One particular thought refused to budge. She'd run through most of her savings to pay her share of the rent already. With Brooke's departure, she'd have to find someone else to share expenses, or she'd need to move to a cheaper apartment.

4

MONEY PROBLEMS AND A SOLUTION

ANGUS KNEW HE WAS in trouble when he glimpsed Holly jogging toward him, blonde ponytail swishing with every bouncy step of her long legging-clad limbs. Memories of the previous night sprinted through his mind, reinforcing his curiosity and his apprehension. How would she greet him today?

"Angus, why are you here?" After a quick glance at him, she averted her pretty gaze. Not shy or uncomfortable. Something else. Her red eyes screamed of a crying-jag.

"I have to train too. You told me you run in the Domain. I figured I'd join you. I also wanted to watch your arse while you run." He fell into step and glanced sideways when she didn't toss back a verbal zinger. "What's wrong?"

"Brooke arrived home this morning. She married Sebastian."

"And?"

"I can't manage the rent on my own."

"Get another roomie."

Holly lengthened her stride as they hit the open fields of the Domain, giving him a glimpse of her butt and the perky blonde ponytail. He increased his pace, breathing deeply to savor the fresh-cut grass scent still lingering on the air from the previous day.

"Truth is, I've run through most of my savings. The apartment is too expensive for me, even sharing. I have to find something cheaper."

Angus shot her a glance, his heart twisting unexpectedly at her distress. "I have a spare room. Move in with me." Impulse drove his reply, but once out there, the thrill of his brilliance grabbed him by the throat.

Her smooth gait faltered, her face contorting into a cute grimace. "No. No, I couldn't do that."

His best guess was he'd rattled her, a fair trade because she was playing merry hell with his sleep patterns. *Steady, O'Neil.* This time his rhythmic steps waned, his brain blasting him a warning to cease his rash inclinations when it came to Holly. Angus scowled. Memories, damn it, got in the way of the good stuff.

"It's a bad idea," she added.

"Why?" When he shoved aside his commonsense, the idea gained velocity. "I'm not there a lot of the time," he continued pushing his point. "Your schedule takes you from Auckland too. If we lived together, we'd manage to see each other more." Impulse firmly in the driving seat again.

"You make it sound effortless. What happens at the end of our relationship?"

"Since there are no emotions involved, we'd remain friends. The future won't present a problem."

She ran at his side, the experience a first for him. He'd never had a girlfriend—correction—friend who fit his interests so well. His wife had bitched about him being away from home and the constant training. Holly understood his commitment to his sport. A plus reason for them to forge ahead.

"I don't know," she said, then tossed her head. "No, it's spitting in the face of fate."

"Think about it for a while."

They fell into silence, passing other joggers—some puffing loudly—and an older woman wearing a blindingly pink tracksuit and leading a boisterous and yappy brown-and-white terrier.

"Does your sister realize you're short of money?"

"No. My parents would help if I asked, but I want to handle everything on my own."

Pride talking. He understood that too. "There's no shame in asking for help."

"Possibly. It's time to do my sprints."

Discussion over. Angus gave a mental shrug. "I'll do

more laps. Do you have training tonight?"

"Yeah. I'm free tomorrow night, though."

Angus laughed. "I'm not. How about Thursday? No, wait. I have a team publicity shoot."

"Thursday's free for me. A light training session on Friday. I'll finish around seven."

"I'll pick you up after training."

"No, I..." She trailed off to bite her bottom lip.

Angus watched her indecision, torn between dragging her into his arms and ordering her to obey. Picking her up after training cost him nothing. "How do you travel to and from training?"

"I catch the train or grab a lift with one of the girls on my team. Wait, you know where I train?"

"Yeah. The netball center, right? Do you drive?"

"Yes."

But a car was beyond her budget. Her flat tone told the story. "I'll let you get on with your sprints. Ring me about moving in, and I'll sort out a key."

AFTER TRAINING THAT NIGHT, Holly prowled her apartment. The tiny rooms seemed like an empty shell, colorless and almost asexual in appearance now that Brooke had packed up the multitude of rainbow cushions, the quirky blue vase that had contained fragrant freesias.

Even the bathroom had suffered a personality scrub. All the cosmetic samples, the sweet-scented perfumes, the hair products. Gone.

Sighing, Holly set about rearranging furniture. She pulled a colorful throw from the depths of her wardrobe in an attempt to stage the place for a prospective flatmate. Her newspaper ad had set the process in motion. Now, all she had to do was wait and screen the applicants. She wouldn't need to panic until the rent fell due at the end of the month.

She crawled into bed close to midnight, her thoughts slipping stealthily to Angus. He hadn't contacted her.

Phone calls about the apartment started after her arrival back from her morning run. One after the other, like a determined netball team, focused on scoring goals.

Ring. Answer. A man. Sorry. No.

Rinse and repeat.

Ring. Ring. *Ring*.

Hadn't she specified she required a female roomie?

Ring. A friend of a teammate. *Yes, at last*.

Holly organized a time for her to see the apartment.

Angus called while she was in the shower and left a message. He rang again and caught her an hour later after she'd seen her teammate's friend plus another apartment-seeker. Neither of them wanted to share a room.

Understandable. The shared bedroom had worked for

her and Brooke, but most people wanted their own space. Friends to sleep over. *A sex-life*, her smartarse mind taunted.

"How are things?" Angus asked.

Despondent, Holly didn't even consider lying. "I had an ad in the paper for someone to share the apartment."

"And?" His tone shifted from friendly-sexy to cool.

"I haven't found anyone suitable. Just a series of creepy guys who can't read properly."

"I told you I have a spare room." Still chilly with a hint of irritable.

"Your offer comes with strings. I don't want to get tangled up and trip over." Honesty. What on earth was wrong with her?

Nah, a new flatmate was the best solution. Accepting his offer was a bad, bad idea. She'd considered his suggestion and discarded it. Again.

"Besides," she said. "Your apartment is gorgeous and way above my budget. How much is your rent a week?"

"I own it," Angus said.

"*Jeesh*, it pisses me off that rugby players get paid more than us," Holly said, too irked to censor her words.

"You know it's relative to sponsorship." He kept his tone even, not jumping to the dangling bait. "The netball league is very new compared to the rugby one."

"You're right." *Apology necessary*. "Sorry, I shouldn't take my frustration out on you."

"Holly, I'll deliver you a set of keys. Come around and check out the spare bedroom whenever you're ready. It's all yours. It's true I'd like you to share my bed, but there's no pressure. Did you touch yourself after I ended our phone call the other night?"

Her chin lifted at the conversation shift, but she didn't miss a beat. "I did."

He made a *tsking* sound, one that hurled lustful messages at her like a wildly misguided netball pass. A shiver rippled across her skin.

"Disobedient." The register of his voice lowered to seductive. "There will be consequences."

A second needy shiver sped through her. Luckily, he couldn't see how that husky voice of his twisted her into turmoil.

She sucked in a breath and reinforced her weak-arse knees. "I need to go. I'm late for work. I haven't had a chance to eat yet."

"You can't keep running away." Now he sounded amused.

"True," she said, thinking of her money problems. They were sure catching up on her in a big way. If she gave up her dream of playing netball, she'd manage fine...

Scowling, she tightened her grip on her phone. She'd chosen to do this for her mother, looking down on her from heaven. She wished to do it for her father and stepmother, who supported her one hundred percent. She intended to poke her dream in the eye and say, "I won."

"Go and eat something. Expect those keys. Oh, and Holly?"

"Yes?"

"Naughty girls get their bottom spanked."

THE KEYS ARRIVED VIA courier early the following morning. She dropped them into her handbag and told herself she'd return them to Angus along with a pretty speech of thanks. Throughout the day, their musical jingle reminded her of their presence, a temptation to stop by Angus's apartment.

"No," she said, her mind wandering while she stood behind the teller's counter and sorted a pile of ten-dollar notes. "Something will come along."

On finishing work for the day, she switched on her phone. Her voicemail was full of messages. By the time she deleted the ones from males, two possibles remained. A return call to her prospective roomies left her right back at the starting line. *Do not pass go. Do not collect a roomie to share the rent.*

As she walked outside via the rear door of the bank and slung her bag over her shoulder, the blasted keys jingled like musical sirens.

"Holy Hannah," she snapped.

"Anything wrong?" a coworker asked.

"No." Holly puffed out a hard sigh. "Just something I need to do." She changed direction and strode to the train station instead of walking home to an empty apartment.

The keys Angus had sent included a note with the security code. She marched up to the imposing building and punched in the four numbers. The marble foyer reminded her of a grand hotel, all gleaming surfaces, and jungle-green plants, the expensive effect enhanced by colored spotlights. Even the air smelled of vanilla and spices. This place was way beyond her wallet, and feeling like an intruder in her bank uniform, she scuttled to the elevator. At the apartment door, she used the key to gain entrance.

Inside, she leaned against the door, taking a big breath to calm her racing pulse. This was the same sensation that grabbed her by the scruff when she messed up, and the umpire pulled her up for contact. Irritation. Determination not to repeat offend. Crap. What choice did she have?

As she sucked in a second breath, she became aware of the running shower. Someone was in the apartment.

Angus shut off the shower and grabbed the nearest towel. If he didn't hurry, he was gonna be late for the publicity shoot. After drying the worst of the moisture clinging to his skin, he stalked from the bathroom.

The soft gasp stopped him in his tracks. His head lifted, and a slow grin curled across his lips. "Hello, Holly."

She averted her gaze and waved with her hand. "You're naked. See, this is why me moving in here wouldn't work."

It'd work fine for what he had in mind, but aware she might do a runner at the slightest provocation, he jerked his head in the direction of the spare room. "Sorry, can't stop to talk. I have a team thing. Make yourself at home. If you're hungry, I made some chicken and vegetable soup in the crockpot. You'll have to reheat it, but it's tasty."

He wandered off, aware of her avid gaze. The urge to waggle his butt was strong, but he resisted. His grin, however, stretched across his face until his cheeks hurt. She'd acted all horrified, but she'd managed a long gawk at his junk before she stepped into her prissy shoes.

He whistled while he selected clothes to wear from the wardrobe—a trouble-free choice that required only part of his mind since he had to wear his team formal uniform. The other part pondered Holly's doings. He stepped into his underwear and trousers, straining to hear footsteps, and grinned at the creak of the wooden floorboards outside the open doorway. She hadn't fled. The jungle-cat alpha stirred at the upped stakes, the prospect of a chase. Color him pleased and purring.

Whistling, he knotted his tie and shrugged into his jacket. Ready to go. A swift glance at his watch confirmed he could spare a minute to stalk—ah, chat with Holly.

He found her in his spare bedroom, perched on the edge of the sole piece of furniture—his father's hand-me-down chair, one he'd tried to toss but couldn't because sinking into its uneven padding wrapped him with happy memories. His last visit home had been months ago. He should squeeze in a quick trip soon. A speculative thought about taking Holly to meet his family had him focusing on her features. She was staring at the view of the Auckland waterfront, her brow furrowed.

"Something wrong?"

"It's perfect," she said. "I can't afford the rent."

"Who said anything about charging you rent? I thought about a tradeoff—"

"Whoa." She scrambled off the chair and backed away. "I told you I'm not that kind of girl."

"Don't jump to conclusions. That's not what I'm suggesting. I wondered if you'd do some housework and the shopping instead of rent. Cook the odd meal. Collect the mail. Water the plants. Take over the stuff I don't get time for because I'm away every other week."

"I'm away too."

"But not as much as me. I prefer someone living here rather than leaving the apartment empty. Besides, it would be nice to come home to someone. That's what I meant by a trade."

"I see," she said stiffly.

"What do you say?"

Holly's shoulders slumped. "I can't continue the way I'm going now."

"So let me help."

"Are you sure this will work?"

"We're friends, right? No messy emotions, just friendship." He sought her gaze and attempted to project a harmless vibe. Inside him, the jungle cat roared in triumph. She was gonna cave. "We're adults. We can handle living together."

There was a long hesitation, and finally—finally—she nodded. "Thank you. I'd love to move in with you, but I'm paying for the groceries."

Satisfaction flooded him, placated the jungle cat, but he restrained his purrs, not wanting to show a hint of anything resembling gloating or sharp teeth. Until he'd experienced her hesitation, he hadn't realized how much he'd wanted her in his home. It'd be hell if she now fled his lair.

"Keep the keys and move in whenever you're ready."

She nodded. "Thanks."

"I'd better go, or the coach and management will bawl me out," Angus said. "Do I get a kiss?"

Her eyes rounded, wariness springing to the fore. Part of her sensed she was prey. *Clever girl.*

"A friendly kiss to seal our deal." She didn't know of his coach's lack of sympathy for lateness, didn't realize she was safe for now.

She approached him with hesitant steps and dived in for a peck on his lips. He stayed her retreat with deft hands at her waist and wallowed in the fragrance of soap and her shampoo. Coconut perhaps? Her gaze darted from his only to return. They stared at each other, silent combatants in a seductive war.

"You smell good," Holly blurted.

"Thank you." His cock swelled, although he ignored the nip of lust, just as he had for long, long, long days this week.

"I should go."

"Coward," he whispered before he lowered his head and took the kiss he wanted.

She gave a tiny whimper as he caressed her lips, then deepened the contact to taste her. Sweet. So sweet. If he weren't on the clock, he'd spend stolen moments sipping from her luscious mouth. Gently, he pushed her away. "I like kissing you."

She stared, signaling hesitation and a range of emotions that flickered across her face like the stop-go motion of a traffic light. "Um..."

"Do you want to spend the night here?"

"No, I'll head home and start packing. If I can get my bed delivered tomorrow—"

"Leave it until the weekend. I'll be away, but you'll be able to get more people to help with the heavy lifting. Talk to you tomorrow," he said, and with another quick brush of lips, he grabbed his car keys and strode from his apartment. In the passage outside, he started to whistle. *All aboard. Excitement ahead.*

EVIDENCE OF HOLLY STUDDED Angus's spare bedroom the next afternoon. Four bags and three cardboard boxes filled one corner. Nosiness had him prying open a bag to reveal two bottles of shampoo. He opened a bottle and sniffed the contents. It was coconut-scented. He replaced the lid and moved on to indulge his curiosity. Conditioner. Other feminine doodads.

Even though he hadn't seen her since the previous night, satisfaction had him whistling a cheerful tune. This relationship was meandering to the bedroom—a slow turtle race to fruition—yet he wouldn't change the pursuit pace. Not a bit. He hadn't enjoyed a chase like this before and found himself wanting to prolong his enjoyment.

He snickered, the sound just a little smug. Toying with his prey. Not very sportsmanlike.

He pulled up in the car park at ten minutes to seven and strode into the stadium to watch the Dynamos train. Their coaching staff shouted advice and instructions from the sideline while a dozen women ran through a zone formation—a pattern of play to keep the opposition players from getting the ball to the goal circle.

"This is a private training. Oh, it's you," an assistant coach said as Angus turned around, prepared to spin a yarn. Her hazel eyes, inquisitive in a round face, dissected him, her square shoulders relaxing beneath her navy Dynamos jacket. "What are you doing here?"

"I'm here to pick up Holly Blackwood. I said I'd give her a lift home."

"Excellent. I don't like her taking public transport home in the dark. The girl is too independent by half."

"Is it okay if I watch the practice?"

"Sure, take a seat over there. Any interruptions, and you're out." Those hazel eyes glinted with promise, and her bulk bore the ability to carry out the threat. "Understand?"

"Yes, thank you." Some teams didn't allow outsiders to watch a training session. His team refused to have strangers around, so he wasn't about to screw up his welcome. Angus backed up his words with a smile of sincerity. The assistant coach wandered off, well-pleased with her work.

A whistle blew. "And again," the head coach barked.

The players ran to their starting positions. The whistle shrieked, and the center zapped the ball to the wing attack. The zone swung into operation, player-on-player, and the wing attack fired the ball back to the center to avoid a held ball—called if a player possessed the ball for longer than three seconds.

Fuck. Fuckety-fuck. That was...what's-her-name. They'd

gone out a couple of times. He racked his brain and came up with Karen. Blonde, busty, and a bully on the court. The attitude translated to a personality flaw off-court, enough to put him off further involvement. She might present future difficulties. He tore his gaze from his past to focus on the woman who summoned his interest now. Holly.

The players moved the ball from teammate to teammate, attempting to force a pass through the wall of bodies created by the opposing players. Angus observed Holly's awareness of the woman she marked, her hawk-like eyes watching the ball's progress like a juicy mouse. All of a sudden, Holly surged, arms outstretched to intercept.

"Damn, she's good," Angus whispered, awe and pride filling him when she snatched the ball mid-air. Respect for a top athlete because that was the line she straddled.

The whistle blasted. "That's what I'm talking about," the coach shouted, pumping her fist above her head. "Great job. Once more, and we'll call it a night. I'll make the team announcement before you leave."

Once they started their warm-down routines, Angus pulled out his e-reader and settled in to wait.

"Angus," Holly said, about twenty minutes later. "I have to stay for the team announcement and have a shower. I'll be another half an hour, maybe longer. It's okay if you can't wait."

"I don't mind," he said, taking in her appearance. Her

long hair was in a tight ponytail, and her face was still pink from exertion. Her T-shirt bore sweat marks, and her yoga pants clung to her lower body. His mind made a sharp U-turn to sex.

"Angus?"

He shook away the fog of lust. "How about we eat at a Viaduct restaurant? Shower at the apartment, and we'll have dinner once you're finished."

"Sounds great. I always end up with a cold shower anyway. Thanks." She jogged away to join a cluster of women on the court.

Angus switched off his reader, surprised by her straightforward agreement. Maybe his charm was working.

A feminine shriek of excitement burst from one woman. The coach was talking, emphasizing her words with vivid hand actions. He searched out Holly and cursed under his breath because her body language screeched with disappointment. She hadn't made the starting team.

The coach finished talking, and the women dispersed. Angus ambled over to join Holly. "Okay?"

"The coach wants to try out new combinations, so I'm on the bench."

"You might still get game time," he said, understanding her frustration and sympathetic because he'd sat in her position.

She shrugged. "Doesn't make it any easier."

"Do you have a jacket? You don't want to get cold."

"Yes, Daddy," she muttered. "It's in my bag."

Her low reply sent signals to his groin. "Fatherly is not how I feel about you."

Her head jerked up, her eyes big and wide and startled. The bloom of her grin and dimples only heightened his predatory instincts.

"Don't treat me like a child then. Won't be long." She raced off to grab her gear bag and returned, her top half now covered by a navy-blue sweatshirt.

Angus grabbed her hand and towed her to the exit.

"Hey, buster." She dug in her heels. "Don't wrench my arm. I need it to play netball."

God, she drove him crazy. He had the worst case of blue balls ever, and the only cure stood in front of him, her chin raised in defiance. "Sorry. Are you ready to leave now?"

"Sure." Holly served him sass in a smile, the type that exerted feminine power. "I'm looking forward to a hot shower."

"You're very trying, Ms. Blackwood."

"And you're bossy, Mr. O'Neil."

He opened the vehicle door for her, then rounded the hood to climb inside.

"Angus! Wait up," a woman called.

He turned to see Carly, another woman he'd dated before calling it quits. The willowy brunette was stunning with a bubbly personality, but her clingy temperament, coupled with her vanilla sexual outlook, had put him off taking their relationship into steady and permanent.

"What are you doing here?" Carly asked. "I knew you'd transferred up to Auckland, but I hadn't seen you around."

"I came to pick up my roomie," he said.

"Who?" She stopped a few inches away from him and lifted her face as if expecting a kiss. When he didn't make the required move, she puckered up and laid one on him. She missed 'cause he turned his head at the last second. She laughed but chagrin reflected in her features. "I didn't know you were seeing anyone."

"Holly Blackwood." And then, because he needed to keep to the script for Holly, he added, "We're friends."

"Holly didn't mention she was living with you." She jiggled her breasts in an enticing manner, a furrow etching between her eyes at his lack of response. "Do you want to meet up for a drink later?"

"Can't tonight," Angus said firmly.

Her frown deepened. "Another night then?"

"Sorry, Carly. Training takes up a lot of my time, and I'm not in Auckland much these days. Nice to see you." *Excuses.* He pressed a quick kiss to her cheek and turned away after a cheerful wave. "Things to do."

Angus slid behind the wheel, braced for questions. When they didn't come, he started the vehicle. "Would you like some music?"

"What have you got?"

"Do you want loud and screechy or something mellow?"

"Mellow sounds good."

Angus hit a button, and a sax wailed bluesy notes.

"I don't recognize it, but that's perfect. Do you know Carly?"

"We went out together a couple of times."

"But you're not seeing her now?"

"Nope, strictly friendly acquaintances. We don't run in the same circles."

She nodded. "I heard you'd come from Christchurch at the start of the rugby season."

"Carly used to play for the Southern team until she moved last year."

"Oh, that's right. Will I meet a lot of your exes?"

"That's rude," Angus said, keeping his tone even. "I've never claimed monk status. There have been other women. I could ask you the same question. You haven't volunteered information about your past."

She wrinkled her nose. "Touché, that was ill-mannered, and I'll try not to do it again. Blame it on past history. I'm sorry, Angus."

"It's okay." Damn, he liked this woman on many levels. At times she was blunt, but she was quick to apologize if the situation warranted. She made him chuckle yet possessed a severe side, and she owned ambition, the drive to succeed in her sport. "There's a brewpub not far from my apartment. They do excellent fish and chips. What do you say?"

"Sounds great. I'm starving."

"Do you want to stay over tonight?"

"I packed my work clothes. They're hanging in the wardrobe."

Angus sent her a knowing look, one that held an edge of humor. "Seems like our minds are driving along the same track. Do you still want to go out for dinner?"

"You left me hanging the other night," she pointed out, all primness with a chiding edge. "The least you can do is feed me the fish and chips you promised."

"Yeah, but you didn't follow my script," he pointed out, slowing the vehicle for a give way sign.

"I bet you didn't either."

"Ah, but that's where you're wrong, Ms. Blackwood. I didn't take care of my banked lust, and my balls are painfully blue." He cast a sidelong glance and chuckled. "Better shut that gaping mouth before a mosquito decides to take it as an invitation."

"You didn't...you haven't?"

Angus turned onto his road and pulled into his apartment parking space. "I believe the word you're seeking is masturbated, Ms. Blackwood."

"You haven't?" she repeated.

"No, which is why I'm eager for our first sleepover." He parked and switched off the ignition. "How did you transport your boxes here?"

"A girl who works with me is interested in my apartment. She drove me home and offered to help me move some of my gear. She's going to bring her boyfriend around to look at the apartment over the weekend."

"That's great. Will they take over?"

"The landlord is Brooke's friend. I'm pretty sure she'll be fine with the switch of tenants. Ugh, I stink. I need that shower."

Angus grinned. "Let's go." The shower test would prove interesting. He'd bet good money she wasn't a woman who spent hours primping.

5

THE PAST WALKS INTO A BAR

HALF AN HOUR LATER, Holly left the apartment with Angus. Both had dressed casually in jeans, jumpers, and warm jackets to ward off the winter night air. A bus trundled down the road, its lights illuminating the dark shadows not reached by the streetlights. The driver screeched around the corner, the bus rumble audible for long moments before silence fell. They'd taken a few steps when Angus grabbed her hand and wove their fingers together.

Holly blinked. "I didn't think tough rugby players liked PDAs."

"I refuse to lose an opportunity to touch you."

"But we're friends. If people see us holding hands, they'll jump to conclusions."

Angus tugged her to a stop and scanned the street.

Empty, aside from one elderly couple. They hunched against the cold and ambled toward the old apartment block at the top of the road. Two drivers had parked their cars on the street, but they sat empty. "I don't see these people you've mentioned."

"You know what I mean."

"Let them think what they want. I won't treat you like a dirty secret. They'll jump to conclusions once they learn we're sharing an apartment, anyway."

"True." Mulling over pluses and minuses hurt Holly's head. Angus-angst was not good for her mental health. "How far is this pub? My stomach's worried my throat's cut."

"Charming."

She shot him a smirk. "Blame my father for the colorful expressions."

"The Drunken Sailor isn't far." He tugged her along for three steps and around a corner before he pointed at the sign depicting an inebriated sailor carrying a tankard of ale. "There, I told you it was close."

She inhaled the curry spice scent coming through the neighboring restaurant door, and her stomach grumbled a complaint. "Yay. Can we order dinner straightaway?"

"Sure thing." He held the door and ushered her inside. Flames that looked real but were probably gas crackled in a fireplace to their right. Not a single chair in the cluster that surrounded the fire remained vacant.

A current pop tune—something girly and flirtatious poured from concealed speakers, and triumphant masculine shouts and contrasting groans came from a group of men playing darts in the far left corner. The scent of beer filled the air, and the faint stickiness of the wooden floor beneath her feet indicated a recent spill.

Angus curved his arm around her waist, subtly directing her steps. "The dining room is this way."

They halted to peruse the blackboard menu.

"Blue cod okay?" he asked. "That's what I'm having."

"My favorite. Can we have garlic bread to start?"

"You remembered I'm not a vampire?"

"Yes." The man amused her without even trying.

"Most men would suspect you're trying to drive them away with this garlic consumption. I'm not that insecure."

"Good to know."

"I'll pay for dinner," he said.

"But—" Her protest died as she caved at his determination. "I'll get the drinks. What would you like?"

"Get me a lager. Whatever the barman recommends."

Holly nodded and made her way over to the bar. She propped her hip against the brass rail and waited her turn for service.

"Holly, baby. I thought it was you." A man's pungent garlic breath blasted her face, the aroma chased by a beer burp.

She retreated until the bar and the woman perched on a

stool beside her halted her withdrawal. "Craig." He didn't seem to notice her lack of enthusiasm.

"I've been thinking about you," Craig boomed.

"You haven't crossed my mind." *Joy.* Halfway to drunk, her ex had hit the hearty stage.

"Bitch."

"Right back at you." Holly turned her back to place her order.

"You here with your sister?"

"No, she's with me," Angus said. "Craig."

"You fuckin' her?"

Holly froze. She'd been wrong. Craig had passed cheery and sailed on to belligerent and arsehole.

"No," Angus snapped. "Mind your manners."

The barman placed a beer and a wine in front of Holly, and she handed over a fifty-dollar note. "Where do you want to sit?"

"Over there." Angus pointed at the area against the wall. "I've grabbed a booth."

"She's a dud in bed."

"No." Holly grabbed Angus's arm when it tensed against her back. "We're not playing his game. Here's your beer." To her relief, he relaxed and followed her to the booth. "Let me tell you a story." Mortified by Craig's behavior, her voice emerged tight and stiff, while her back felt like a board, darted by the fascinated gawks from other bar patrons.

Behind them, the barman growled a warning. "Craig, take a seat and shut the hell up, or I'll get security to escort you from the bar."

"She's not worth it anyway," Craig snarled.

"Our dinner won't take long. We have time for a story."

Angus sounded matter of fact, and Holly's tension receded. Good to know he wasn't a dumb hothead.

A waitress delivered the garlic bread, the scent flinging her back to the bar and Craig.

Holly dropped onto the padded seat and slid into the booth. Now that she was on the other side of the pub, heat suffused her cheeks, and her hand had developed an irritating quiver. She balled her fist and hid it beneath the table, but one stolen glance at Angus told her he sensed her anger and unease.

"How do you know him?" Angus shunted the garlic bread to her, and she plucked a piece from the plate. A task to occupy her hands.

"I met him through Brooke and her friends. He plays rugby for Auckland." Craig hadn't made the first team this year, which had to rankle, and no doubt accounted for his shitty attitude. She bit into the bread, the ooze of butter and the garlic setting off a rumble of hunger.

"Do you have personal knowledge of him? As in if he wears boxers or briefs?"

"He goes commando most of the time."

"I see."

"We used to date. It didn't end well." An understatement. Boyfriend number three, Craig, hadn't reacted well to her calling him out on his cheating. "He possesses a loose concept of monogamy. Our ideas of a relationship didn't gel."

"I see."

"Will you stop saying that?" she snapped.

Angus's impassive expression cracked into a wide grin. "Look, the guy is an ass. I know that, and I don't even play in the same team. He's the sort who strikes out with his fists rather than using his brain."

"I learned that firsthand. A guy doesn't get to cheat, then slap my face because I question his morals."

"Bastard." Angus half-stood, his furious gaze zeroing in on Craig.

"And my friends don't get to fight my battles. Stand down. Craig had a shiner for a week, and I'm unsure how long the swollen balls lasted. My father taught me self-defense. I've never been a girly girl like Brooke. We might have the same father, but we received a fair portion of genes from our respective mothers."

Angus settled again, and a slight smile curved those sensual lips of his. "You hit Craig?"

"Yeah, I know I shouldn't have sunk to his level, but he pissed me off. He tried to press charges."

The kitchen called their meal number, and Angus rose. "Stay there. I'll get our dinners. Do you want ketchup?"

"Yes, please." Haunted by boyfriends past, Holly closed her eyes and considered Angus. Another rugby player. With her history, their relationship wouldn't end well, yet stupidly she'd gone one better, burning her bridges and moving in with him.

A plate thudded down.

"Don't overthink the situation," Angus said in a cool tone. "I'm nothing like him. Besides, we're friends. You are not my significant other."

"Gee, I hate that term. I mean, what does it indicate? Everyone's so PC these days."

Angus chuckled, his long legs jostling hers as he slid into the booth. "Girlfriend wasn't quite right because you're both."

"Maybe fuck buddy?"

"Not accurate," he said. "Although I'm hoping we get to change that tonight."

The sensual gleam in his eyes snared her, and she couldn't refute his charisma. She swallowed, nerves scrambling through her belly even as she nodded her acceptance. "Works for me."

Angus studied the battered fish and crispy chips on his plate. "This looks delicious, but I'm tempted to go without dinner."

Holly speared her fish with her fork and cut off a chunk with her knife. "If you think I intend to leave this meal untouched, you have rocks in your head. I enjoy eating, and I missed lunch."

"Nibble on me."

Holly's gaze slid across his broad shoulders and she snorted. "With the amount of training you do, you'd taste as tough as an old gumboot."

"I feel mildly insulted."

Holly giggled. She pressed her fingers to her lips. "Oops, I can't even blame that on alcohol since I've only had two sips."

"The fish is excellent."

"Yes, it is." She dragged a thick-cut chip through a puddle of ketchup.

"Why did you miss lunch?" Angus asked.

"I had to leave work early. My boss gave me permission, but I had to work through my break." Tara had stated other things as well. Unemployment things. Holly tried to ignore the metaphorical ax, even though its blade gleamed dangerously in her future. She needed the job at the bank. If—no, *when* she left, she'd have to walk straight into another position. Money problems sucked.

"You shouldn't miss meals. Take an energy bar or something."

"I have a couple in my bag, but I can't eat while I'm serving on the counter. It was busy today. I never had a chance to duck out and snatch a couple of bites."

They continued their meal until two guys from Angus's team came over to say hello. Holly had met them through her ex-boyfriends and at parties. Curiosity transmitted from them in waves.

"Move on, folks," Holly said with an elaborate gesture. "Two friends eating dinner together. Nothing to see here."

Angus chuckled. The two men grinned and good-naturedly wandered away to join their friends and report back.

"Men are worse gossips than women," Holly said.

"Probably."

Holly finished the last of her fish and dredged her remaining chips through the ketchup left on her plate. "That was the best meal I've eaten in ages."

"Must be the company," Angus said.

"That too," Holly agreed.

"You ready to leave?"

Holly smiled. "More than ready."

They slid out of the booth and left the pub, waving at friends and acquaintances. Outside, Angus snared her hand, and it felt so right, Holly didn't bother to argue.

They entered the apartment, and Angus turned on the lights while they shed their coats. "Do you want something to drink? A coffee? Another glass of wine?"

"I'd like a kiss. We could proceed from there." It was refreshing not having to play games and wonder how to behave or what came next. This arrangement with Angus meant upfront and honest when it came to her needs.

"Works for me." He tugged her along the passage and

into his bedroom. "We might as well start our kissing in here because I intend to head to a mattress next. Any objections?"

"Not a one."

A light flicked on, and the king-size bed loomed in front of them. She took in his bedroom with a swift glance. Not a single pair of underpants or other dirty laundry decorated the floor, and he'd made his bed after leaving it this morning. Loose coins lay on the bedside cabinet, plus a paperback—a bestseller.

"You're reading *Fifty Shades*?"

"I was curious."

"So that's where you discovered your spanking interest," she said, amused and a trifle disappointed too. The idea of him punishing her in that way had heated her body when she'd thought his idea was an original one.

"No, it's not from the book. I have my very own ideas about what I want to do to you, with you." His eyes gleamed, and he morphed into an alpha male, not that he'd behaved like a sissy to start with, but now she was ultra-aware of him, of being alone in a bedroom and at his mercy.

"I see." Her breasts lifted with her slow, deep breath. The air hissed past her lips again, and lust reared its serpent head, arousal shimmering through her veins to settle in heavy expectation at the juncture of her thighs.

He tugged her hand, and she stepped willingly in his

direction.

"I haven't forgotten my promise," he whispered. "Although I intended to save it until later. If you'd prefer to take your punishment now…"

"Oh, no." Holly spluttered a laugh and backed up as far as his grip allowed.

"You think I'm kidding."

"I think we should keep spanking between lovers," she said. "Loving swats have no place between friends." The man got to her on so many levels. Tempted her. *Yep, she was toast, well-done to a crisp.*

"I disagree." He jerked her to him, sin and sexiness stamped in his features.

She hit his chest and let out a soft *oomph*. Before she could utter a word, his mouth closed over hers, firm and confident. His arms wrapped around her shoulders, holding her in place while he conquered her and left her feeling dainty and feminine. Desired. She surrendered to his expertise without hesitation, her arms lifting to clutch his shoulders. He tasted of beer and garlic, the thought making her want to giggle—no lurking vampires in this bedroom.

Fever filled her—desperation for more. Damn, the man possessed skills. A few touches, some kisses, that kick-arse confidence directed her way, and she turned to girly putty.

He lifted his head, his gaze a spell she was powerless to resist. "Too many clothes. Can I undress you?"

She nodded mutely, and he raised the electric blue-and-black jumper over her head to hit the black mesh top beneath.

"Woman, you're wearing too many clothes."

"I was cold. Besides, I don't want to get sick and have to make myself unavailable to play."

His face softened. "How does this come off?"

"Over my head."

He peeled off the tunic top and crouched to unzip her boots.

"Now that's where I like to see my men—kneeling at my feet."

"Spanking," he said without glancing up from his task.

She clapped a hand over her mouth, but it didn't mute her glee. A muffled snort escaped.

He lifted her feet one at a time and tossed her boots and socks aside. He unzipped her jeans and tugged them down her long legs. Then he grabbed her and sat on the bed, placing her over his knee seconds before her *eep* of surprise emerged. She kicked and tried to wriggle free, but her jeans tangled around her feet, hampering her efforts. His hand slapped on her buttocks hard, the crack of palm meeting flesh startling her more than the smack. Another two followed in quick succession, and a burst of searing pain streaked through her.

"*Ow!*"

"Are you going to kick me in the balls when I let you

up?" he asked.

"Depends," she said, the throb in her buttocks morphing into edgy heat.

"Hmm," he said, his hand caressing her bottom over her lacy undies. "You have a smart mouth. You doubt my intentions and imply I'll be an arsehole if we decide to go back to platonic friends. I think you need a couple more swats to drive home my sincerity. We *will* make fantastic friends."

Holly looked over her shoulder and winked. "You've given me more than enough to think about."

Angus stroked one butt cheek, his hand generating more of that jittery thrill in her. He tugged down her panties, baring her butt to his gaze. Her skin prickled, a renewed surge of fire striking her pussy. This time his finger trailed over her naked arse and crept toward her sex. She bit her bottom lip, fighting to remain still even though every particle in her body cried for her to turn into his arms and demand he take her hard.

Whack. Whack. He spanked her again, the angle of the blows shifting, the sharp crack of pain that came with each strike transforming to warmth. She bit back a moan even as, weirdly, instinct had her butt lifting into his next smack. He stopped, and her skin prickled. She knew he was studying her pink flesh. A prickle darted through her, pushing dark craving to the fore.

His fingers traced over her tingling buttocks again and

down the backs of her thighs. On his finger's return journey, her breath caught in acute anticipation. *What's he going to do for his next move?*

"You look pretty in pink," he murmured. His fingertips lingered at the spot where her thighs met her buttocks, teasing her with a repetitive caress. She swallowed. Edginess filled her now, the desperate need for more. Her tongue darted out to lick her lips while she pondered the right words to get her what she wanted. Blunt had worked so far, but he was proving unpredictable, keeping her off balance. The wretched man.

His thighs shifted as he helped her stand. Big hands cupped her hips and propelled her to face him. "Okay?"

The tip of her tongue retraced her lips, snagging his attention. "My butt hurts."

"Can you lie on your back?"

"Yes." Unsure of what he wanted and uncertain of how to react, she stared at him with a silent question.

"Lie back and spread your legs."

Okay. Holly followed his instructions, her heart rate jumping as cool air washed over her aching core.

He stripped, not shifting his gaze from her for an instant.

Holly's skin tickled all over, and she was ultra-conscious of the moist heat dampening her folds, of his calm focus. He gave away none of his thoughts, but she was wet and horny. *His fault.* She opened her mouth to complain and closed it again. Perhaps mouthing off wasn't the best idea.

Instead, she peeked at him, drinking in the wondrous sight. The man—he looked even better without his clothes. Her fingers itched to explore his broad chest and the toned, muscular ridges of his torso while she imagined twining her limbs with his long legs and bulky thighs. Her gaze dropped to his cock and the rampant thrust of his shaft. She moistened her dry lips and thought about how he'd feel gliding into her mouth.

Holly swallowed and redistributed her weight on the bed. A twinge of pain from her bottom reminded her of the spanking, and conflicting emotions—guilt, pleasure, and confusion—charged together like players in a rugby scrum. This...Angus...was outside her comfort zone. Perhaps she should reconsider their arrangement.

"What now?" she asked when the heavy silence scratched her nerves past rawness. The thump of her heart increased to a loud drum as she fought the urge to bound off his bed, to run.

"Spread your legs wider. Yeah, like that," he said on her compliance.

His face still offered no clues, and when he moved, she flinched.

"Steady, sweet pea. I won't hurt you." He bent and pressed a kiss to her mound.

She hissed, the warmth of his lips like a quick jolt of electricity. She stared at his shaggy black hair, her muscles tense while her mind bustled with questions. What did he intend to do to her?

He trailed a line of kisses along the join of her thigh and torso, so soft and quick they made her squirm. She recoiled as he reached out, her mind a jumble of uncertainty.

"Just grabbing a condom. I'm not gonna hurt you."

She gave a jerky nod. Although instinct told her to flee, curiosity would make her stay, that and the writhing need lashing every erogenous zone. Her body hungered as if she'd starved it of touch on purpose.

Angus murmured something she didn't hear, and before she could ask, he lifted her butt and dragged his tongue the length of her slit. He circled her clit and massaged the tiny nub. It swelled under his ministrations, exhilaration roaring through her at the suddenness of his move. A throaty moan sounded, the raw need it contained astounding her.

"Angus," she whispered, drifting her hands lower to clasp his skull.

He stopped, lifted his head. "Hands at your sides. Don't touch me."

"I...what?"

"I'm the one directing here. I decide what happens next."

Say what?

"Holly." The starkness of his tone jolted her, made her realize she still fisted her hands in his black hair.

She let go, their gazes connecting. The silent challenge in his sent lust zipping through her veins even as she wondered how to handle him to get what she craved.

"Holly?"

Without haste, she placed her hands at her sides.

Warm approval washed away his cool disinterest, and her heart did a little shimmy of excitement. He lowered his head again, a stream of air drifting across her clit. Another twist of sensation grabbed her at the caress of his breath over her aching flesh. Her hips jerked upward. Ah, contact. A satisfied sigh whispered from her, and he chuckled. The lazy stroke of his tongue filled her with bliss, and she drifted, her eyes shut to savor better everything he did to her.

His head lifted, and a groan of protest escaped her. Her eyes flicked open, and she searched him out. "What?"

A grin flashed. "Eyes open, sweet pea. I need to see your eyes whenever I look up at you."

"Sure." *Whatever.*

He waited for a beat before going down on her again. She stared at his head between her legs, shivered at the suction of his mouth. Her hips canted upward again, seeking deeper contact. He chuckled against her flesh and increased his assault, adding his fingers to the mix. One finger slid inside her, curled, and hit a spot that made Holly gasp and twitch. The finger stroked back and forth on the tender flesh while his mouth and tongue worked her clit.

"Angus." His name was a plea. *Get me off now.*

The pulse at her throat beat a rapid tattoo, the orgasmic buzz swelling within her, growing bigger, better. Holly fought the urge to close her eyes, struggled with it until Angus glanced up with such approval she gulped and battled against her eyelids closing even harder.

His finger stroked, and his mouth closed over her throbbing nub and sucked. The sensations yanked her under without warning—a storm of pleasure. It dragged her into the undertow then snapped, leaving her in delectable agony.

"Hands under your head, babe. Now."

"Sweet pea. Babe. You should decide," she muttered, but she did as he requested and kept her eyes wide open while the remnants of pleasure rode her.

"Which would you prefer? Sweet pea or babe?" he asked in cool interest. The crackle of a foil packet tore her attention from his face. She watched his nimble fingers handle the condom, position it, and roll the latex down his length. "Are you gonna answer or keep staring?"

"Keep staring, I think." Fascinated, she studied his erection. He handled the thick length with an ease that told her he was used to women and comfortable with his body. A liquid roll of desire shot through her. She'd bet the man had skills and looked forward to more firsthand experience.

Angus crawled over her, his eyes serious again. "What if

I decide to try a few out for size, work out which one suits you best?"

He pressed his forehead to hers, and she caught his flash of devilment before she could no longer focus because of his closeness. His lips brushed hers before he pushed into her—one long glide until he buried his shaft to the hilt.

"Damn, you feel amazing. You okay?"

"More than okay," she said. One of her hands shifted and reached for him.

"*Ah-ah*," he admonished. "Put the hand back."

"Do you have an aversion to touching or something?"

"My rules. My way."

"And if I don't obey?"

"I stop, or you get another spanking."

"No." Unwilling to test him, she returned her hand to the required position. She'd experience his lovemaking tonight and come around his cock if it was the last thing she did. Later she'd challenge him and see what happened. Her butt tingled at the memory of the spanking. Strangely, the blows had felt pretty good after a while.

"Good girl."

"Another one," she said drily. "I like to think I'm mature enough to qualify as a woman."

"Yes," he said, withdrawing from her body and torturing them both with a slow retreat. "You are most definitely a woman." He slid home again, turning the hunger between them razor-sharp. He rested his weight on his hands, and the only place they touched was at their groins. While their bodies were separate now, his concentration on her was total. He drove inside her, his pectorals bulging with each thrust, his hips flexing. Never was the fine delineation of his muscles more apparent—his ridged abs and flat stomach.

"I've wanted to do this since the moment I saw you at the pub." He shoved into her hard, the stroke rough, but she took every thrust with pleasure. "My next favorite fantasy was you with your red lipstick-covered mouth around my dick and my fingers wrapped around your hair."

"But you've waited to make a move."

"Delayed gratification. Besides..." He glanced at where they joined, watched the glint of her juices shining on his shaft.

"Besides what?"

"You talk too much," he said firmly. "Quiet."

"So many rules," Holly muttered, but she stopped talking and relaxed to enjoy the heck out of his skilled moves. He drove into her, the drag of his cock hitting a sweet spot. She arched in silent demand, and his pace increased, propelling them both toward a climax.

A streak of pleasure grabbed hold, wrapped around her senses. She groaned and wanted to tell him that maybe rugby players weren't as bad as she'd thought. But she gave in to the bliss, letting him get on with his seductive plundering.

He was so skilled at it.

Her eyelids fluttered, and she gasped at the erotic snap of her nerve endings. Gradually, she came back to herself, her body humming with residual satisfaction. Boneless, she watched his harshly drawn face, their gazes connecting as he seized pleasure. When his body stopped shuddering, he dipped his head to take her lips, this time as if he were worshiping her mouth. He dropped his weight onto her then rolled, parting their bodies. He dealt swiftly with the condom and tugged her against his chest.

"So now you cuddle," she said.

"I wanted to see if you could follow orders."

"A test?" Holly twisted to read his expression while weighing his words. Sex with Angus—talk about different. With Craig, she'd been lucky to come at all unless she took care of her orgasms.

"Of sorts. I'm particular about the women I sleep with."

"Meaning what?" If he insulted her, she was out of here.

"Some women don't like me taking charge in the way I enjoy."

"Oh." Well, he'd been bossy, but he hadn't been a selfish lover. "I came twice. You'll be my best friend if you manage that every day."

His lips twitched. "So you don't have a problem with my orders?"

"Not from my end. Am I allowed to touch you now, or do you have some sort of phobia I should know about?"

"Touch me as much as you want." He lifted her hair away from her shoulder and dropped a kiss on her collarbone. "Is your bottom sore?" One of his hands roved over her hip to cup her butt.

"A bit."

"I have some cream to take care of the bruising."

"I have arnica cream in my gear bag," she said. "I'll apply some later." She pushed her hands against his chest. "Just for the record, my breasts are sensitive, and I get hot if my partner starts there."

Angus rolled flat on his back and grinned up at her. "I'll keep that in mind."

"Good," she said crisply. "Any hot spots I should know about?"

"Honesty and faithfulness are a big turn-on for me. Be upfront with me at all times, and we'll be fine."

Holly nodded and straddled his hips. "Same goes. I'm going against all my rules by hooking up with you. Don't make me regret my decision." *Oh, yeah. Brave words, Holly.* She hoped she wasn't setting herself up for heartbreak.

She feathered her fingers across his chest, testing his firm pectoral muscles with her palms. He had a little chest hair, not too much, but enough to make her sigh with appreciation. She edged down his body and smiled on feeling the firm press of his cock. "Do you have more condoms?"

"In the bedside drawer."

She nodded, her fingertips mapping his muscular abdomen, the dip of his belly button, and the direction of his happy trail. "It's fun touching you."

"Torturing me, more like," he said.

"Turnabout is fair play. Has anyone spanked you?"

He snorted out a belly laugh. "No, and don't think you're going to be the first. I'm in charge here."

"Yes, sir."

His eyes darkened, and the sensual gleam she was coming to know lit them with a glorious blue. "Use it or lose it, cupcake."

"Cupcake? And rugby talk? *Ooh*," she cooed, but taking his warning to heart, she kissed his hipbone and tested his six-pack with her teeth. A shudder slid through his muscular frame, and when she lifted and curled her right hand around his shaft, he let out a hiss. She pumped up and down, watching the ruddy crown with interest. Already pre-come leaked from his tip, and she dipped her head to lap at it with her tongue.

"Take me into your mouth," he said, his tone leaving no doubt in her mind. It was an order rather than a suggestion.

She took her sweet time until he growled. Grinning, she opened her mouth and sucked him deep, then gave quick flicks of her tongue against the sensitive underside. The muscles of his stomach flexed, and he lifted his hips, pushing his cock deeper. He speared his fingers into her hair and loosened her ponytail.

"More tongue," he directed, tugging at her hair, but not so hard that it hurt. "I like that. Babe, remember the eyes. Watch my face."

Holly groaned around his cock and almost gagged when he pushed a fraction deeper. She jerked back, her eyes watering as she watched him. Pleasure glowed in his features, his approval ratcheting up strange sensations in her. She took him deep, using her tongue to stroke his slit and tease more pre-come from him.

He trembled like a green virgin. "Holly, yeah. Just like that. God, that feels good."

The smart-Alec part of her wanted to chide him about closing his eyes, but the feminine part was pleased to provoke this reaction. Seeing him lost in his pleasure made her long to satisfy him even more. She withdrew, took him back, using every bit of her expertise to make him feel great. Again and again, she sucked him inside the heat of her mouth, massaged him with the flat of her tongue, turning herself on while she watched his bliss-filled face. She caressed his hard balls and gloried in his pained groan. Shifting slightly, she was all too aware of her wetness and the need spiraling inside her. His cock seemed to swell, and he cried out her name seconds before hot ejaculate shot down her throat. He gripped her head, his cock pulsing for long moments while he held her in place.

She swallowed and pulled back a fraction, sucked in

some air, and tenderly licked his softening cock.

"Holly," he whispered, releasing his grip to stroke her hair. "You are incredible. Come up here."

Holly sighed and crawled up his body until her cheek pressed against his chest. His hand smoothed over her back and came to rest on her butt. She failed to hold back a wince.

"Climb under the covers so you don't get cold." He left the bedroom, and she stood. Which side did he sleep on? He reappeared shortly afterward, a tub of arnica cream in his hands. "I thought I told you to get in bed."

The idea of his hands stroking her bottom—heck—looking at her backside made her want to squirm. "Aye-aye, sir." She gave him a saucy salute and sashayed around the bed foot to her favored side.

"I should spank you again," he muttered, coming up behind her and directing her back to the other side. He tugged back the duvet. "In you get."

"I like the right. I can't sleep on this side."

"By the time I'm finished with you, you'll sleep."

She knew better than to challenge him, even if his stern tone tempted her to pull a comical face. It also raised awareness. The sensation skated through her veins, tugging at her breasts. She squeezed her thighs together, wanting to prolong and increase the enjoyment pulsing through her.

"In you get." He gave her butt a soft slap, and she yelped.

"Lie on your front."

She shot him a dirty look but complied, resting her chin on her folded arms and closing her eyes. His cool fingers trailed across her rear, and she flinched.

"Steady," he said in a soothing voice.

The chill of the cream made her recoil, but the gentle way he rubbed it in calmed the heat in her buttocks. She relaxed under the pressure of his hands, letting out a purr of contentment. The man had moves—accomplished on the rugby field and skilled in the bedroom. If she weren't careful, he'd change her views on rugby players, and then she'd land in the middle of a trouble storm.

6

BAD NEWS DERAILS PLAN

ANGUS WOKE WITH AN armful of woman and an enticing orange and lavender perfume filling his lungs. Confused at first by her warmth and the tangle of sheets around his legs, he froze until images of the previous evening flickered through his mind like an erotic movie. Then he smiled in a lazy cat-caught-his-prey grin. In his usual bossy manner, he'd led proceedings, and he'd deviated far from his plan of plain vanilla sex. Instead, he'd eased Holly in a direction to assuage his cravings. Instinct had driven him to wield his hand in the promised spanking.

Yet despite that, Holly was still here in his bed. She hadn't run screaming into the night or replicated his ex-wife's actions by screeching he needed therapy. Even better, she hadn't mentioned leaving but had drifted to sleep at his side.

He checked his watch and made out the time despite the lack of light in his bedroom. Half an hour until the alarm. The muted sounds of traffic outside told him the world was waking even if Holly was still dozing.

"Sweet pea," he whispered, easing aside strands of blonde hair to bare her neck. He pressed his lips to the tender skin behind her ear and chuckled when she moaned. "Time to wake."

Her breasts were warm to his questing touch, the nipples full. Unable to resist, he turned her onto her back and sucked one into his mouth. Using his tongue, he teased the peak until it firmed to a hard nub and watched for a reaction. God, she smelled so good with a trace of that coconut shampoo and her lavender and orange, and even better, she bore his scent. The idea pleased him more than it should.

He waited for a distress signal to toll that he was one and done with Holly. Nothing happened apart from his growing desire to take her again. He paused for a beat longer. Not a breath of danger blotted his mental horizon.

Well, hell. Somehow, she'd *really* hooked his interest, a trick other women had tried and failed. Amusement flooded him at the irony since the stubborn woman kept trying to push him into friend territory.

Curiosity had him imagining Holly in his future, and it wasn't difficult to picture her fitting into his life. He inhaled and pushed the breath back out again. Somehow, the woman had slipped past his guard, and he wanted her something fierce. Something to consider...

Now that she'd engaged him, he'd chase, seduce and do everything in his power to keep her around. He wanted rockin' good, rockin' hard sex with Holly for a long, long time. His gaze traced the curve of her hip.

Still mostly asleep, Holly shifted, her legs splaying. Perfect. He moved his attentions to her other breast and ran his palm along her torso. Her skin was soft, like the petals of a rose. His hand came to a rest on her mound, and she remained unmoving.

"Holly," he whispered.

A tiny protest came from her, and he wished he could see her better.

His fingers skated down her crease, and when dampness greeted his touch, he fingered her clit. A breathy sound escaped her, but her eyes remained closed.

"Wakey, wakey, sunshine." Angus continued playing and slid one finger inside her channel. When she still didn't rouse, he added another finger and angled them to hit her sweet spot. Without warning, she jolted. Her eyes snapped open, telegraphing confusion.

"Ah, you're awake," he whispered.

"What's the time?" she mumbled, the tension oozing from her muscles.

Grinning, even though she wouldn't see in the darkness, he said, "Not long until the alarm."

"Wanna sleep."

"But I have a problem." He grabbed her hand and placed it on his morning wood.

"Go away."

"I promise to do all the work."

"Men," she muttered, but she didn't tell him to piss off again, and that cheered him no-end.

He fumbled for a condom and didn't find one. With a curse, he finally discovered one on top of the nightstand behind the lamp. After rolling on the rubber, he rose over her and guided his cock to her entrance. He pushed inside her scorching passage and tortured himself with a leisurely thrust until her clinging flesh encased him in glorious, wet heat.

Gradually, her arms looped around his shoulders in a loose embrace.

"Thank you, babe."

"Angus," she said with asperity.

Grinning because she sounded awake now, he covered her complaint with his mouth and set about turning her to his point of view. Unhurried strokes into her pussy. Languorous kisses. He lifted his head and sought her expression. It was still dark, but her eyes gleamed in the dim light.

"Fucking you is amazing, Holly. The way your sweet pussy clings to my cock. Pure magic. This arrangement is a great idea."

And it could become more, he mused. He'd give the idea some thought and see how things panned out between them. Once Holly relaxed and came to trust him fully, she might understand the potential between them. All he knew was what he had with Holly—even in these baby stages—was ten times better than what he'd had with his ex. He was himself instead of pretending to be someone less driven, less sexual as he'd been forced to do with Louise. His gut told him he and Holly could have something special, *had* something special. Yeah, he'd give this situation more consideration.

"Angus." She yanked his ears and diverted his attention back to her. "Start moving again."

Angus withdrew and thrust into her with more force. He repeated the move. "Better?"

"Much." She lifted her hips to meet his strokes.

"Touch yourself," he ordered. "You need to catch up."

"Just for the record. I'm not good in the mornings. I work on automatic pilot until I start running. The exercise wakes me."

"This is exercise."

"A little less talk, a bit more action."

Laughing, he took her mouth with distraction in mind. It worked, and even better, she followed his instructions, getting busy with her hand. The stroke of her fingers against the base of his dick pushed him closer to climax. He fleetingly thought of Louise and how she'd have told him to piss off. Evicting the past, he kissed Holly, grinning at the faint taste of garlic.

Holly's fingers maneuvered, grazing his shaft again. His balls tightened, lifted, and the buzz of orgasm boiled in them.

"You need to hurry, cupcake."

"Cupcake?" The motion of her fingers halted. "Really?"

"Better than pudding."

"Don't you dare. Angus, oh, oh..." she trailed off, and he felt the rhythmic pulses of her sex clutching at his cock.

Just the signal he needed. He stroked into her a little more vigorously, a tad faster, and nanoseconds later, he exploded so hard he saw starbursts behind his closed eyes. Slowly, he came back to himself. He clasped her to him and brushed a kiss across the tip of her nose.

Across the room, his radio burst into life, the signal to move.

"Now, isn't a fuck better than the alarm clock as a wake-up call?"

Holly muttered under her breath—something rude, no doubt—and humor spread in him like a swift ball passed along a backline. He withdrew and climbed out of bed to deal with the condom and alarm.

"Up and at 'em, pudding," he said. "I have time to run with you before I leave for the airport."

"Airport?" Holly swung her legs over the edge of the bed and stood, stretching her arms above her head.

"I'm flying to Melbourne today, then on to South Africa for two weeks. Remember? Our away games," he said, masculine appreciation at the fore.

She turned to face him, all curves and temptation. "You're away for two weeks?"

"Yeah, will you miss me?" *Gorgeous view.*

"No."

Angus grinned and grabbed a pair of boxer-briefs. "I'll miss you."

THE APARTMENT SEEMED TOO spacious without Angus. Too lonely. Too silent. Holly flicked on the radio and waggled her hips to a top-forty hit. She'd moved the last of her stuff out of the old apartment yesterday, and now on Sunday morning, she was busy making the spare bedroom her own, or at least unpacking boxes. Piles of clothes and a stack of books covered the top of the bare mattress. She placed a lavender candle—a gift from Brooke—on the wooden dresser and checked her watch, wanting to leave time for a grocery run before she headed to the stadium.

"Note to self," she muttered. "Avoid the magazine aisle and ladies' periodicals featuring pictures of Angus and his team with beautiful women."

Her cell phone rang, and her heart did a happy skip. The excitement faded when she glanced at the screen. Not

Angus, but then he was busy. She could always break down and email the address he'd left for her in his note of instructions.

The phone jingled again, this time sounding faintly impatient. She scanned the screen. Botheration. She still hadn't worked out what to tell her parents.

"Hi," she said, filling her voice with cheeriness.

"Holly," her father said. "Your mother and I thought we'd come to the game tonight."

"I'm not in the starting line-up. The coach is still trying different player combinations."

"But you'll play at some stage?"

"I think so."

"Good enough." Approval came down the line. "We'll drop in at the apartment. Maria thinks you girls don't eat enough, and she's been baking up a storm. We can give you a lift to the stadium. See you—"

"Dad, I've moved. A friend needed a house sitter, and he has a spare room, so I took him up on his offer. I'll give you the address." If she boggled her father with a flurry of words, he wouldn't counter with difficult questions. "It's a great place with views over the harbor. It's also closer to training, and I save on travel time."

"He?"

Holly screwed up her nose. Trust her father to pick past her bullshit. "Yes, he's a friend of Brooke's and plays for the Auckland Dragons."

"I thought you'd sworn off rugby players. That's what your mother said."

"Dad." Holly was glad he wasn't standing in the same room because a blush heated her face. "It's not like that. I have my own room. Angus and I don't see each other very much because we're both training and playing away games, and I have work—"

"Maria thinks you're working too hard. We watched your last game on TV, and she thinks you look pale."

"I'm fine, Dad."

"Where is this new place?"

Holly rattled off the address even as she wondered how to find the time to sort out Angus's spare bedroom—her space. At first, it'd been easier to sleep in Angus's bed because of the boxes stacked on every surface. Now, she was more organized, but she still hadn't moved into her own bed. She was trying hard not to analyze her delay or examine her behavior too closely—the intimacy of using Angus's bed when he wasn't present or the fact that she missed him. "See you later, Dad. It will be good to see you."

She hung up, scowled at the mess, released a huge sigh and got busy. She found her father and stepmother waiting for her when she returned from the supermarket.

"Look, Keith. I was right. Holly is pale, and she's lost weight." Maria was the same height as Brooke, and mother and daughter looked like sisters with their blonde hair, blue eyes, and broad smiles. Their chattiness further likened them.

"She looks the same to me." Her father grabbed Holly in a tight embrace. He was tall like Holly, his hair a light brown and now peppered with gray. He'd retained his fitness and figure working on their block of land, despite Maria's need to feed everyone.

Maria elbowed him out of the way and brushed her fingers over Holly's cheek. Concern shaded her features. "Are you eating a balanced diet? You're not eating junk food?"

Holly winked at her father and grinned. "I'm eating properly, although I won't refuse home baking. Did you make gingerbread?"

Maria gave Holly a swift hug. "Of course. Do you want to have an early snack before the game? I can make something."

"There's a nice pub down the road," Holly suggested.

"I brought some soup and herb bread," Maria said. "Would that work? I'd prefer to catch up without interruptions."

Just what Holly feared. Maria wanted to *chat*. Somehow, she'd given herself away. The woman had worked as a reporter in another life and had a nose for a story. "Well, come inside. Do you want me to carry something? I have one free hand."

"Good idea," her father said. "Maria packed a lot of food."

Holly shared a knowing grin with her father. She'd lucked out in the stepmother stakes and gave thanks regularly. Maria was the best. Not only had she made Holly's father happy, but she'd made them into a family and given Holly a fantastic older sister.

"Oh, Holly," Maria said on entering the apartment. "What an incredible view."

"I told you it's a great place. Would you like a tour?" The cleaning service had visited yesterday, and the apartment sparkled like a fine jewel.

"Yes, please. Will we meet your flatmate?"

"No, he's away with games in Melbourne and South Africa for a couple of weeks." *Thank goodness*.

"Why haven't we heard about him before?" her father asked.

"Yes, why did you decide to move? You could have found someone else to share if you thought you'd feel lonely."

"There was one bedroom, Mum. Sharing with Brooke worked, but a person I don't know? Think about the potential problems."

"She has a point, Maria," her father said.

"Besides, most people who came to view the apartment wanted privacy, and I don't blame them. What if they wanted a boyfriend to stay for the night?"

"But you're sharing with a man," Maria said.

Holly shook her head, suppressing her laugh. "Brooke spent more time at Seb's apartment than ours."

"But she's married now," Maria said, her brow furrowing in a way that told Holly her other daughter worried Maria too.

Holly pulled a face. "I don't have time for a man. Heck, sometimes it feels like I'm a rodent on a wheel, sprinting to keep up with my schedule. Why would I add more stress to my life? And a rugby player." Her nose wrinkled even as she spiced her expression with a tiny grin. "Been there, tossed the T-shirt."

"You're doing too much," her mother fretted.

"No, I'm living my dream," Holly said. "And I have to work hard to get to my ultimate destination."

LATER THAT NIGHT IN the stadium, Holly sat on the reserve's bench and watched the play of the ball. Still in her warm-up uniform but already wearing her lucky socks, she itched to get on the court.

"Go, Dynamos!" a young, dark-haired woman shouted from the stand behind Holly.

Rubber-soled shoes squeaked against the flooring. Players urged each other on and shouted to attract attention if they were free to receive a pass. The odd grunt interspersed the furious pace when players collided.

Holly sucked in her breath as one of her team chucked a lazy pass. She inhaled a faint hit of a menthol rub that one of the players must've used to help with sore muscles, her mind registering the scent as she focused on the play.

The Western Gazelle's wing defense leaped for an intercept, plucked the ball from mid-air, and whipped it to her teammate with dizzying speed. Holly groaned along with the crowd. Seconds later, the umpire blew his whistle, signaling an opposition goal. The Dynamo fans remained quiet, the cheers coming from the Gazelle section of the stand.

The hooter resounded for halftime, and the Dynamo coaching staff gathered around Holly's team.

"We're ten goals down," the head coach said. "We can take this game back, but we need to move the ball faster through mid-court. You're overthinking your passes, and your hesitation is giving the Gazelles time to intercept the ball.

"Right, position changes. Claire, you're on at goal attack, Rachel wing defense, and Holly, I want you to go on in goal defense. Questions?"

Yay, lucky socks. Pleased to finally take part in the action, Holly performed her stretches to warm her muscles again. The hooter blared, and she ran on with her team, psyched to get game time.

"Are you living with Angus O'Neil?" Karen asked.

Holly sent her an impatient look because their team was about to take the center pass. They needed to focus.

"Are you?"

"Yes."

The umpire blasted on her whistle, and play commenced. Holly darted forward, keeping pace with her opposition player. Man, the goal attack was fast. The woman was also tall and solid and sneakily slammed into Holly each time they contested the ball. And worse, she shot goals from all over the circle, unfazed by Holly's marking and defense.

Don't get impatient. Keep with it.

She stuck to the woman, refusing to get rattled, refusing to make a stupid beginner's mistake, refusing to avoid contact. Bruises were a small price to pay. *Make the most of this chance.*

The ball headed in their direction.

Holly watched it the entire time, gathering herself to leap. Her opposition jumped too and popped out a hip, jostling Holly off-balance.

Holly stumbled back, then lurched forward when someone shoved her in the back. Grunting, she crashed to the floor, landing in an ungainly heap.

She had to get up. She needed to grab the ball.

Holly twisted, pushing up on her hands and knees. *Eek, she was bleeding. They'd need to wipe the blood off the court.*

Hurriedly, Holly attempted to stand and fell back with an agonized groan. Stabbing, piercing, burning pain seized her ankle, traveled up her leg.

Dimly, she heard the whistle blow to halt play.

With tears shrouding her vision, she cradled her ankle. God, it hurt. And worse, she didn't think she could continue playing.

"You pushed her," someone said.

"I didn't mean to. It was an accident," a woman replied.

Holly couldn't identify the speakers, not when surrounded by a forest of feminine legs.

A female medic squatted beside her. "Your ankle?"

Holly blinked to clear her sight. "Yeah."

"Can you move your foot? Your toes?"

Holly flexed her foot and tried to muffle her whimper.

The medic probed her ankle with careful fingers. "Looks like a sprain. Can you stand with my help?"

Holly gave a quick nod, even though she wasn't certain. The medic took her arm, hoisting her to her feet. The slight weight on her injured ankle sent fiery jabs up her leg. A hoarse sob rippled up her throat. *Damn.* Holly swiped a hand across her cheeks and gave in to the truth. No way in hell was she gonna walk off this injury.

"Steady," the medic said.

Every muscle in her body ached in sympathy. She sniffed. *No more crying.*

"I know it hurts, Holly. Can you make it to the sideline?"

She bit her lip and hobbled off the court to the cheers of the crowd. With the medic's help, she sank into a chair.

"Let's take off that shoe." The medic eased off Holly's

shoe and peeled off her white sock. "Hmm, a bit swollen. Just give me a sec, and we'll get some ice on it."

The head coach squeezed Holly's shoulder. "A sprain or worse?"

"Looks like a sprain, but we'll get a doctor to confirm and take X-rays." The medic left and returned with an ice pack. "This should help reduce the swelling."

"How long will I be out?" Holly asked, wanting to get the bad news done with first.

"Up to six weeks." The medic's gaze held sympathy.

Holly's shoulders sagged. "Six weeks?"

"Could be longer. It depends on how your ankle responds to treatment."

"Okay." Holly winced at the icy chill of disappointment. Off-court hours meant she'd have no chance of impressing the selectors. Tears slid down her cheeks. Her dreams of playing for the national team had just bounced away like a misdirected netball.

"I CAN STAY WITH you," Maria said, following her into Angus's apartment later that night. They'd picked her up once she'd finished in the x-ray department. "Keith, tell her. She shouldn't stay alone."

"Thanks, but I won't be good company. Besides, there are only two bedrooms. I can't let you use Angus's bedroom without asking him."

Maria scowled, anger flushing her cheeks. "That woman pushed you. I still say the umpire should've sent her off."

"She's on my team. It was an accident. Karen didn't mean to knock me over," Holly said, maneuvering on the crutches they'd given her. *Her lucky socks had lost their magic.*

"Come home and stay with us," her father said.

"Thanks, but I'll still need to work," Holly said, although how she'd manage with crutches was a mystery. "Please, don't worry. I promise if I need help, I'll ring and ask."

Maria gave a grudging nod. "All right, but I'll be ringing you every day to check on you."

"Call us if you need anything." Her father's voice held gruff affection.

The telephone issued a summons, and Holly used her crutches to cross the room. "I promise I'll call. Thanks for coming to see me play." She picked up the phone. "Just a sec," she said into the speaker. "Honestly, Mum, I'll be fine."

"I'll drop by to see you tomorrow," Maria said in a no-nonsense voice.

"Keep safe," her father said. "And lock the door as soon as you're off the phone."

"Yes, Dad." Holly bit back a tired grin at the familiar order. Her father didn't trust city dwellers and preferred the slower pace on his lifestyle block in Clevedon, south of Auckland.

Once the door clicked shut, she shifted her attention to the phone. "Hello. Sorry to keep you waiting."

"My, my, honey. Aren't you polite?"

Some of her depression lifted at the husky tone. "Honey?"

"You don't like honey?"

"I love honey on toast," she said.

"Pity. I'll have to keep trying. How did the game go tonight?"

Holly hesitated. "I was on for five minutes. I landed in the wrong place, and the other players jostled me. Took a spill and sprained my ankle."

"Shit, I'm sorry," Angus said. "How bad is the sprain?"

"Not as bad as I feared. The doctor told me to rest my ankle, elevate, and ice. You know—the usual stuff." Her throat tightened, and she had to force her next words past a lumpy obstruction. "Worst case scenario—the doctor said I might be out for up to six weeks."

"Damn."

"Yeah. How about you? Meet any sexy women over there?"

"One or two, but I prefer you."

"Silver tongue," she said, attempting a grin and failing woefully. "Is your training going well?"

"Yeah, I'm on the team."

"Great, I'll watch your match on TV. Friday night, right? Early Saturday morning here."

"Yeah. Holly, I know you're disappointed. I wish I were there to hug you."

His sympathetic words made tears leak from her eyes, and it was with relief she heard voices in the background calling his name.

"I've got to go, sweetie. There's a golf ball calling my name."

She blotted at the stubborn fall of tears with a handy tissue. "I bet it's not calling you *sweetie*."

"Not that one either? I'll have to give the subject more consideration. Talk to you in the morning."

"You don't have to worry—"

"I'm not," he broke in. "I want to...to make sure you don't sleep in late."

"Good night, Angus."

"Good night, babe."

Holly set the phone back on its charger and, using the crutches, hobbled to her bedroom, tears sliding over her cheeks. This injury sucked, and the timing made her want to kick and scream and curse at the unfairness. All her sacrifices for the season now meant nothing.

7

TENSION IN THE HOME CAMP

THE FOLLOWING DAY AT eight-thirty, Holly maneuvered carefully through the bank with her crutches. Somewhere a phone rang and stopped. She nodded a greeting to the other tellers but didn't halt to chat or answer their questions.

"I have an appointment with Tara," she said and kept moving.

One teller pulled a face while the other sent her a sympathetic smile. Tara wasn't the most popular woman at the bank because she was severe and literal and by the book.

Using crutches took fortitude, and right now, Holly wasn't feeling anywhere near qualified for sainthood. The ache at her temples thumped in rhythm with the throb in her ankle. Grimacing, she halted to place her weight on one crutch and knock on her boss's office for entry. A private chat with Tara was always stressful, and the bothersome dryness in Holly's mouth refused to leave, despite repeated swallowing.

"Come in."

Holly inhaled and wiped her sweaty hands on her black trousers before opening the glass door. She limped into her boss's office, tilted off-balance, and by luck hit the leather visitor chair instead of landing on the floor on her arse. The office was immaculate with the usual arrangement of seasonal flowers—this vase containing white lilies with a sweet aroma.

Tara—a thin, pale woman with ruthlessly tamed black hair—finished perusing the printed spreadsheets on her glossy desk before lifting her gaze to study Holly with her usual impatience.

"I've sprained my ankle and can't come into work," Holly blurted. She held her breath and wished, for once, she could have a conversation with her boss without feeling as if she'd committed an unpardonable crime.

Tara pressed her pink lips together and scowled at Holly for long seconds. "How long are you off? Do you have a medical certificate?"

Bitch. She could've asked how the injury had occurred. Holly tugged the certificate from her pocket and handed it over. "The doctor gave me the week off work and instructed me to keep off my feet."

"Fine," Tara said, her tone implying it was anything but okay. "Your timing is lousy. We're already a teller short."

"It was an accident," Holly said tersely. Hell, she'd give almost anything for a healthy ankle right now.

"Keep me apprised of your progress," Tara said and turned her attention back to her paperwork. "Shut the door on your way out."

Holly bottled up the tirade she ached to fire at her boss. Damn, she needed another job. Instead, she rose unsteadily to her feet and navigated her way out, her muscles protesting every step of the way. The deep purple bruise on her hip and the lesser ones on her ribs—caused by player contact—complained with each jerky step. The two painkillers she'd swallowed half an hour earlier weren't shifting the dull discomfort. She wrestled the door shut with a noisy thump and limped over to where Maria waited in the customer portion of the bank.

"Everything okay?" Maria asked, her mouth pursed on seeing Holly's tight expression.

"Not really."

"*Ooh*, that woman," Maria said. "I take it Tara still hasn't forgiven you for beating her out on that spot in the high school netball team."

"No." Holly sighed. "The woman bears a mean grudge."

"You won that spot fair and square," Maria said. "You're younger, but you have more talent than her, and that's why the coach pulled you out of the junior team."

"Thanks, Mum." Maria had championed her from the start and treated Holly the same as Brooke, right down to matters of discipline.

"All part of the service, dear. What would you like to do now?"

"How about coffee and a cupcake at the Domain tearooms? I'm going to buy a newspaper and check out jobs. I'm tired of Tara's petty behavior. Life is way too short to put up with her crap. The doctor recommended a physiotherapist for my ankle after the swelling subsides. I need to ring for an appointment."

Maria gave her a bright smile of approval. "An excellent plan. I'll treat you to morning tea, and we'll search the jobs together."

Two weeks later

Angus unlocked the door to his apartment and dragged his suitcase after him. It was the middle of the day, and silence greeted him along with cookie spices. Cinnamon and nutmeg. Disappointment surged through him because Holly wasn't here, but she'd be at work.

A women's magazine sat on the counter, one with his face on the cover. He winced, and his attention shifted to the bottle of prescription painkillers. Some of his joy at arriving home faded. Holly hadn't mentioned her ankle, and he hadn't liked to prod the emotional wound when he couldn't be with her in person to sympathize.

During their phone calls, she'd told him she was going to physio and resting. She hadn't spoken of her frustration, but it took little imagination to know how he'd feel in the same position. Pissed. Angry. Discouraged. He'd want to put his fist through the nearest wall.

What made it doubly hard was the fact he'd played out of his skin in South Africa, racking up two brilliant man-of-the-match games. The national selectors had attended the matches, and he was hoping he'd done enough to attract their favorable notice. There was no way to share his excitement with Holly without making him feel and sound like a heartless bastard.

Angus unpacked his bag, chucked on a load of washing, and popped a capsule in the coffee machine. The gurgle of the machine cycle and the scent of coffee became the backdrop while he opened his mail.

A key in the door had him turning with alacrity. A smile formed, and excitement and eagerness expanded his chest along with a trace of anxiety. Had their separation changed anything? The door opened, and Holly scampered in, using her crutches like a pro.

"Angus, when did you arrive home?" She halted, her mouth curling into a welcoming smile, and his tension eased, his shoulders relaxing as he basked under the warmth of her grin.

He took three giant steps and wrapped his arms around her. The crutches got in the way and fell to the floor. "I've been home about an hour. Did you work today?"

"Officially, I'm on extended sick leave, but unofficially I attended a job interview."

His brows rose. "Yeah?"

"Yeah, and I got the job. It's still banking and is in a call center, which isn't far from here. They don't mind working around my netball commitments, and the wages are better. Plus, my new boss seems lovely." She beamed, and his heart turned over with a wave of affection.

God, he'd missed her. He hadn't looked at another woman while in South Africa, hadn't wanted to, and his teammates had teased him, telling him he'd lost his mojo. "What plans do you have for the rest of the day?"

"I have to ring my parents and let them know about the job interview. After that, I might make some popcorn, pour a glass of wine and watch a movie."

"How do you feel about an afternoon nap after your phone call?"

Her eyes widened, then she offered an impish grin. "I'm not up to acrobats or anything kinky."

A chuckle escaped him, along with a surge of relief she hadn't let depression grab hold. It couldn't have been easy, and he respected and approved of her positive mindset. "I love a mind-reading woman."

"You say that now since it works to your advantage."

He lowered his mouth and took possession of hers, savoring and teasing her lips until she opened on a soft moan. God, she felt so right in his arms. He'd missed this. *Her*. Hunger deepened the exchange, and when he lifted his head, they stared at each other, both breathing hard. "I can work around your ankle." He pressed her hand against the hard bulge of his erection. "See what you do to me, pumpkin?"

She snorted at his endearment, as he'd known she would.

"Pumpkin is the worst one yet."

"Really?" He pretended disappointment. "I'll need to try harder."

"Let me grab my crutches," she said.

"You don't need them." Angus swung her into his arms, savoring her warm weight and the spicy orange blossom fragrance coming off her skin. It lacked the usual hint of lavender. "New perfume?"

"Yes, Mum brought it for me last week. A surprise present."

"The best kind," he said, thinking of the soft teal-and-cream scarf he'd purchased for her in South Africa. He couldn't wait to see her wearing his gift—the scarf and nothing else. His gut bucked, and desire flared hotter and more urgent.

"Yes. And on that note, I'd better ring Mum about the job. She'll be anxious to learn how the interview went."

Angus set her down and waited while she made her call.

Once she'd finished, he scooped her up again and carried her into his bedroom. He set her on the middle of his bed, his gaze wandering every part of her—the sparkling eyes and faint color in her cheeks, the neat braid with the escapee wisps around her face. Cute dimple. "I'm going to undress you. Okay?"

"And this time he asks permission," she said with a teasing smile that gripped him by the cock and yanked him deeper into...something dangerously foreign.

He wasn't positive where they were going, and for once, he didn't care—as long as they ended up together. "Normally, I'd tell you to do it and watch each sexy move. Today, you get a pass. I'd hate to hurt you."

Pain flittered over her face—the emotional-about-to-cry kind—prior to her flashing him a bright smile, brittle at the edges. "The ankle is healing well. The doctor and the physio are pleased with my progress."

"But you're antsy." Angus unbuttoned the feminine pink and white blouse. "I understand the impatience to get back to your game." He nuzzled the valley between her breasts and took a quick nip. "But we both know going back too early might come back to haunt you later." He shifted her body to unclip her white bra and pulled it down her arms. "Pretty. I missed you."

She wriggled and sighed, the puff of air warm against his cheek.

"You don't have to sound happy about it." He drew off

her black trousers, then her plain white cotton panties. Once she was naked, he sat back on his heels and gazed his fill. "You look and smell so much better than my tour roomie." He ran his hand over her shoulder and stayed it on the slope of one breast.

"If you're going to tell me I feel better too, you'd better step away. We'll have coffee instead."

"Hey." He prevented her open amusement by kissing her. She flicked her tongue against his, her manner provocative. A heavy pulsating sensation settled in his groin. He tore his mouth away and savored the picture she made. "You're beautiful. I missed having you around."

"Thanks, but you don't have to say that. I'm a sure thing."

Angus bit back a pithy curse and plucked a condom from the drawer instead. He was a sure thing, too. Happy skimming the relationship's surface, she didn't understand the surprising and growing depths of his feelings. Hell, part of him was shocked at the instant click between them and his urge to push for more intimacy. But Holly was honest and genuine and didn't flirt or play feminine games. He admired her drive, her love and respect for her family, her willingness to work rather than expect parental handouts. This, plus the qualities and quirks he'd noticed during the time they'd spent together so far, had cracked his protective shell and made him yearn for more.

A mistake? He wasn't sure, but time would tell.

He slid a hand across her belly, gloried in her quick gasp. He caught her next sound with his mouth and parted her legs with his knee. Liquid heat greeted his hand, and when she arched into his touch, he acknowledged their separation had irked him. In such a short time, she'd dug into his life, his mind, the irony being she wanted nothing except friendship. *Damn*. If he didn't get his mind on the job, she'd move on, anyway.

Angus settled in to kiss her again, deep and explicit, while he palmed her arse. A soft cry escaped her, and he breathed easier when she clutched his shoulders. While she mightn't have noticed his absence, she'd missed the sexual sizzle. Pleased at this, he nibbled a trail down her neck, over her collarbone to settle in at her breast.

"Suck." She tugged at his hair to guide him. "Please."

"I aim to please you," he said, swirling his tongue around her nipple then sucking it into the heat of his mouth. He tortured the peak to a tight bud and repeated the sequence with her other nipple.

"Angus." She rocked against him in silent demand.

Wet, swollen folds greeted his questing fingers. He swept a finger over her clit, applying the slightest pressure. Her fingernails dug into his back, the sensual digs speeding straight to his balls. "Condom. I'll embarrass myself if I don't get inside you soon."

"I'm ready." Her wink displayed sass and dared him to hurry.

His hand shook as he rolled on the condom. Then he was pushing into her hot flesh and savoring the snug grip around his cock. He stared into her eyes, the connection between them snapping into place and twisting his heart.

"I've dreamed about this for days." He pulled back and powered into her again. He kept up the rapid pace, driving them both hard. Hot gasps filled his ear, and their lips met when she jerked his head down to claim his mouth. A quick punch of heat swamped him, her lush body soft to his hardness. Angus tried to slow, tried to savor, but urgency pushed him fiercely. He drove deep, an animal sound of pleasure scorching his throat. Damn, this was good, so perfect. Angus stroked into her and exploded, coming so fast that bright colors flickered behind his eyelids.

Fuck, he'd closed his eyes again. Weird. He liked to watch the woman he was with and insisted she watched him in return. His world had shifted since he'd met Holly.

"Hey, buster," she said, wriggling beneath him. "I thought you were taking care of everything."

He grinned as he slipped a hand between their bodies. "You'll have to think of another name. Buster doesn't do it for me."

"I'll call you Big Ears if you don't get me off soon."

Chuckling, he did some precision work on her clit and took her mouth in a devouring kiss. She turned liquid around his softening cock, sent an intense burst of heat swirling through him. Blood crowded his dick again. God, he needed another condom. He gave a shallow thrust and twisted his hips.

"Yes, yes, yes!" Holly issued a ragged shout, her eyes wide open and on him. He saw her honesty, the pleasure twirling inside her, and it turned him to mush. He strummed her clit, soothing this time, caught her scream with his mouth and felt a distinct shift in his heart.

The pulses tailed off, and she went boneless. Angus pulled out of her, making sure he didn't lose the condom. After discarding it, he drew Holly into his arms and pulled the covers over their naked bodies.

"I missed you." He reiterated his earlier words, wanted to give her honesty.

"But we hardly know each other," she said into his shoulder.

Some of his pleasure dropped away with his smile. Damn, the woman. "We know enough." He dragged in a quick breath, trying to wrangle his rising displeasure. *Softly, softly.* "Are you doubting my sincerity?"

She lifted her head to blink at him. "What?"

"Do you think I saw other women while I was away?" He met her puzzlement with a full-on glare.

"No, of course not. At least I didn't hear any rumors."

"I didn't. I wouldn't." Angus rolled away and stood, frustrated with Holly's throwaway words about rumors.

His ex had constantly jumped to conclusions, the

green-eyed monster inside Louise causing tension between them. He opened drawers, yanking out the first clothes to hand while he told himself to exercise patience with Holly. She didn't understand his growing fascination with her because he hadn't told her he wanted more. He hadn't wanted to scare her when she was so man-shy.

"If I stay here, I'll go to sleep. It's best to wait until my normal bedtime," he said in a poor explanation of his rapid departure. She was going to think he was a nutcase, but he needed space to think. "Ah, I might go for some fresh air."

With a final glance at a confused Holly, Angus strode from the room and paced the kitchen. Despite the jetlag, edginess kept him moving. He grabbed his running shoes, found a pair of socks, and seconds later left the apartment at a run.

Walking away from Holly was the obvious answer, but gut instinct told him that was stupid. A huge mistake. They'd be fantastic together if she pushed past her determination not to have another serious relationship. *Hell*. When Holly didn't think too hard or let the past get in the way, everything about their liaison worked fine. But, he couldn't blame Holly for all of this situation. The trouble was his impatience, his growing need to tell Holly of his feelings...

His feet slapped the pavement, echoing his dissatisfaction. Hell, his sexual urges didn't scare her, and they were more than compatible in the bedroom. Who the hell would've guessed history would screw everything up for them?

As he rounded the waterfront and headed for the footbridge spanning the marina, the rain started to fall. Hard, fat drops struck his face and stung his bare arms. Angus ignored them and kept running toward the Viaduct with its busy restaurants and bars, the press of people. Clearing his head and soothing his ragged feelings might take time.

HOLLY STARED AT THE door, the slam still resounding through her mind. Her throat ached, and when she attempted to stand, her knees almost folded.

Men always cheated in the end—at least her experience showed her they couldn't keep their dicks in their pants. She supposed she should've aimed for tact, but at the start, she'd told him a relationship between them wouldn't work. Yet despite that, sentiment precariously close to guilt roared to life. Beneath his strange behavior, she'd witnessed a flash of hurt.

A tight ache filled her chest as she reached for clothes. Her bra and fitted T-shirt were unproblematic. Donning her cotton panties took a concerted effort, and she gritted her teeth, her balance precarious. By the time she'd pulled on her sweats, perspiration dotted her forehead. She hopped along the passage to the kitchen to prepare a cup of peppermint tea. Minutes later, she inhaled the mint from the steaming cup, hoping it might relax her. It didn't. Instead, the thud of the winter rain blasted the roof, and the wind wailed, increasing her anxiety.

Two hours later, Angus stalked inside, water dripping off his hair and chin.

"I'll get you a towel," she said, struggling to her feet.

"I'll get it," Angus barked.

Okay. Holly dropped back into her chair and pretended to watch the television when her gaze remained glued to him. She needed to apologize. Heck, maybe she should explain, so at least he understood why she was having trouble with trust.

In the distance, the shower started. Holly scooped up her crutches and hobbled to the kitchen. The rubber tips squeaked against the tiles with each careful step. She put on the jug to make another pot of tea—Earl Grey this time.

"We need to talk," Angus said as soon as he entered the room, now dressed in an old pair of jeans, almost white with age. A blue T-shirt stretched across his broad chest, the color echoing in his eyes and making them impossibly bright.

"We do," she agreed. "I made a fresh pot of tea." When she started to rise, he stayed her with his hand signal.

"I'll get it." Minutes later, he returned with two mugs of tea, hers with a slice of lemon floating in the top.

The sight of the lemon made her realize how Angus noted the small things. He took care of her without making a big deal of it. She tugged at her collar, feeling even guiltier at her earlier careless words.

"I have not, and I will never cheat on you," Angus said, his blue eyes sincere with his conviction. "If there ever comes a time when I want out of our relationship, I'll have the guts to tell you face-to-face."

"But—" Holly bit her lip before another tactless reply made enough room to shove her foot inside her mouth. She'd been about to state the rumors about him and other women—the stories in the magazines must have a factual basis.

"But what?" His eyes were hard, his attitude demanding the truth.

Her chin lifted. "There are rumors about you and lots of women."

He made an impatient sound, half curse. "You'll have to make up your mind, Holly. Either you believe me, or you don't." He paused and sighed. "I'm sorry for snapping at you. You didn't deserve it. Chalk it up to tiredness on my part."

"It's okay." Holly closed her eyes, acknowledging the truth of the part before his apology. He was right, damn it. "I've had three serious boyfriends since I left school. None of the relationships ended well, and they might have colored my perceptions about men." Bother, now she sounded defensive.

"And?"

"I'm sorry, Angus." Her heart sank. She was making a mess of this.

"Craig plays rugby." He took a sip of his tea, his expression turning thoughtful. "Were the others rugby players?"

"I play netball. That means I socialize with many people who play sports." And there was that defensive note. *Again*.

"I see." Angus's tone remained even.

"What do you see?"

"I play rugby."

"Yes." This time caution echoed in her reply.

"You're painting me with the same brush."

"I-I'm not. Not consciously." Her attention shot to her feet, settled on her bandaged ankle while her heart raced in a rapid tattoo. Now she was lying, and he sensed it. Damn, she had to fix this, stop panicking at the shift and deepening emotions of their relationship. Because she'd missed him—talking to him and seeing him. She'd counted the days to his return.

"I know what I want from our relationship. When you decide what you want, let me know." He stood. "I missed you while I was away, and I don't want to argue. What do you want for dinner?"

Grateful for the olive branch, she said, "I've taken out a

pack of stewing steak. Mum brought me a tagine pot, and I thought I'd try it out. Dinner won't take long once I get the vegetables chopped and the spices cooked off." That was a new one—a man who didn't sulk. "I don't want to argue either."

"Excellent. Dinner sounds good. I'll help."

Holly nodded, pleased at the gesture of reconciliation. She stood and picked up her crutches.

Angus frowned. "Why don't you sit at the breakfast nook and give me directions? You should rest your ankle as much as possible."

One glance at Angus told her it wasn't a suggestion. She gave a curt nod, even as she silently acknowledged this was his thoughtfulness appearing yet again. "Thanks."

Soon the scent of onions, cumin, and coriander wafted through the kitchen. Angus carried out her instructions with a competence she hadn't previously witnessed in a man.

"I watched your games on TV," Holly said. "You played well."

"Some games just flow, and everything clicks."

"And sometimes they suck," she said ruefully. "Still, the coach asked me to go to the Sydney game this weekend, so they haven't written me off."

"How much longer do you need the crutches?"

"I wanted to toss them a week ago. The physio talked me into babying my ankle for longer."

"She's the expert."

"He," Holly corrected.

"How's the pain level?"

"It throbs if I overdo things."

"How are you going to get to work?"

"The call center for my new job isn't far from here. I'll either walk to work or grab a cab if I can't handle the distance. The physio said I can start some gentle walking soon."

"That's great."

"Yeah." She glanced at the recipe on her tablet and worried her bottom lip. "Add one can of chopped tomatoes, a handful of cranberries, and the chopped pumpkin."

Angus added the ingredients. "How long does it cook?"

"Half an hour on low. We need to add the chickpeas after twenty minutes."

Angus lowered the heat on the gas and fitted the tagine's conical lid. He set the timer. "A glass of wine while we wait for dinner?"

"Sure."

His tone was still cool, and it made her feel as if she'd broken something precious. Mending the rift might take more effort than she'd thought.

Later that night, Holly hesitated, unsure whether she should join Angus in his bedroom or sleep in her room for the evening. She dithered, trying to decide.

"Shit. Damn. Fuck," she muttered. She paused a moment longer before grabbing a pair of pajamas from a set of drawers in her room. After changing into them, she picked up her crutches and tap-tap-tapped a path to Angus's bedroom.

He was already in bed, his bedside lamp switched off. The lamp on Holly's side of the bed still glowed with a soft golden light. Relief tore through her as she set her crutches against the wall and slid into bed. This rift between them was fixable, and she found she wanted to mend it. That told her that maybe she liked Angus more than she'd planned on at the start of this relationship. She arranged her pillows and turned off the light, plunging the bedroom into darkness. Beside her, Angus was already asleep, the long flight catching up on him.

While he played rugby professionally, he differed from her previous boyfriends. He was considerate and looked after her. He seemed genuine, and she liked him a lot. She had to remember his good points and give him a chance, instead of tarring him with Craig's misdeeds.

She must've fallen asleep, and she woke with a heavy masculine arm draped around her waist. Warm lips nuzzled her neck, took tiny bites.

"What are you doing?" she asked in a drowsy voice.

"If you don't know, I mustn't be doing it right. Why are you wearing pajamas?"

"I wasn't sure if you wanted me to share your bed last

night."

The lips stilled at her throat. "For the record, I always want you in my bed. Naked," he added. "Take them off before I decide you need another spanking."

Her sex gave an insistent pulse. Weird. Every time he mentioned spanking, or she thought about the punishment, her pussy turned molten hot and damp. She slipped the cotton pants off, tugging her bikini briefs down at the same time. With the pants dropped on the floor, she turned her attention to the pajama top.

"I'll do it," he said.

It was still dark in the bedroom, and Holly had no clue of the time. Angus ran his hand under the hem of the top, his warm palm going straight to one breast. He cupped it, holding the weight in his hand while his thumb strummed the nipple. A hard flick against the tender peak made her jump, the quick surge of sensation traveling like a bungee to her belly. He sought her other breast with his mouth, taking the nipple through the cotton of her top. The friction of lips and cloth sent another shot of pleasure crawling through her veins. A throaty moan escaped her.

She wriggled in a silent demand for more, the heat from his attentions settling in a hard ball of lust between her thighs.

When he raised his head, she cried a muffled protest, her breast aching for his touch.

"Soon, love," he said. "Let me get this off so I can touch

your skin." He made quick work of the task, leaving her side to retrieve a condom. His bedside lamp clicked on. She heard the crinkle of the wrapper, the soft grunt he gave as he worked the latex up his shaft. He thrust into her, his body a welcome weight.

One hard thrust seated him, the hot, wet slide of his cock caressing her internally. She wanted to close her eyes, to wallow in the pleasure, the excitement slamming her body with every stroke.

"Holly."

Just the sound of her name made her want to obey him. She sought his gaze, registered his approval, his flare of hunger. He drove inside her again, and the growing tremors made her cry out, lift her hips to make the most of each erotic plunge.

"That's it, buttercup. Let me steal your breath," he whispered as he cupped one breast. His fingers tugged Holly's nipple, then gave a hard pinch.

The twinge of pain rocked her body, frisking her nerve endings.

Laughing at her moan of appreciation, he continued to play her body with a skill she valued but would probably worry about later. Pleading words backed up in her throat, stubbornness holding them back even as she played the game she'd started with eyes open wide.

"Are you ready to come?" he whispered, hot intent blazing from him.

"Yes. Oh, yes."

He caught her cry with his mouth, sliding his tongue past her lips as he quickened his thrusts. Up he drove her. Higher and higher, the pressure climbed inside her. She balanced on the narrow border between pleasure and pain until he powered into her yet again. The clawing tension snapped, and with a sob of surrender, she convulsed around his cock.

Angus thrust inside her with furious strokes, prolonging her ecstasy. He shoved into her a final time with a hoarse groan and buried his face against her neck. She held his trembling body tight and luxuriated in the aftershocks.

This was enough for now.

There was no point stressing about the future, worrying about what Angus might or might not do. She'd only wear herself out and take her mind away from the things that were important to her—healing and her netball.

8

SECRETS ARE INTERESTING THINGS

"I HAVE TO GO to a sponsor's party tomorrow night," Angus said the next morning as he strode into the kitchen. "Will you come with me?"

Holly looked up from her fruit and cereal. "Is it formal?"

"Afraid so. Do you have a practice?"

Her first instinct was to cry off, invent an excuse. Instead, she thought of everything Angus had done for her, and she nodded. "There is, but I won't be doing anything except listening to strategy and learning the new zone we're trying. I'll check with the coach."

"Thanks. We have to arrive at the hotel at seven to schmooze with the sponsors as they arrive. The other wives and girlfriends are attending. You won't be alone while I'm doing my thing with the sponsors."

"No problem," Holly said. "I know several of the wives

already." While social occasions weren't her favorite thing, she'd do her best to help Angus.

On Friday night, Holly walked into the Palace Hotel on Angus's arm, garbed in her best red dress. A fresh flower bouquet and designer perfumes blasted her when they entered the function room. A male pianist sat at a grand piano, providing background music, and soft laughter and chatter floated in the air. As she'd assumed, she knew the players on Angus's team, and most of the girlfriends and wives were acquaintances. Each plus-one wore gorgeous gowns—primarily black and slinky—and had impeccable makeup. Thank goodness for the dress her sister had given her. It helped her to fit in better.

"Well, aren't you two full of secrets?" a familiar voice said from behind her.

Holly jolted at the recognizable and slightly mocking tone. She turned to face her sister. "Brooke, when did you get back from your honeymoon?"

Brooke sported a light tan, emphasized by her figure-hugging white dress and upswept blonde hair. She radiated happiness.

"This morning," Brooke said. "Seb promised the club he'd be here for this shindig. I rang your cell, but you had it turned off. I don't get why you bother having a phone since it's never on. I told you the halter dress looks better on you than me. Red suits you, and you've listened to my makeup tips. Nice job. Do a twirl for me." Contentment made her sister even more talkative than usual.

Holly completed the requisite spin and thought about her answer regarding the phone. *Money*. She had little and skimped where possible, which meant she turned off her phone.

"Can we sit together, or is there a seating plan?" Holly asked.

"Don't change the subject. I want to talk about you and Angus." Brooke caught the nosy interest in their conversation from bystanders and dragged Holly over to a quiet corner. "Spill."

Holly grinned even as she prepared to play the role of an Academy Award-Winning actor. "Angus and I are roomies. He needed someone to monitor things while he's away, and I offered to help. The rent is much cheaper." She kept the explanation concise, aware too much chatter would give the game away.

Brooke's brows drew together, displaying her obvious disappointment. "Nothing is going on between you?"

Holly rolled her eyes. "You know my position on rugby players. Angus is a friend and nothing more."

But that didn't mean she enjoyed seeing one of Brooke's single friends hanging off Angus's arm two hours later. A scowl tugged her mouth as she watched the woman drag Angus onto the dance floor after dinner and the formal speeches. Holly's fingers twisted together and tightened beneath the table while she worked on replacing the frown with a smile and focusing on the chatter at her table. She even added to the current conversation regarding next weekend's game.

Inside she continued to simmer, her hands squeezing imaginary necks out of the sight of other diners. The worst part was her inability to share her irritation without creating gossip. They'd told everyone they were friends and flatmates, and a jealous incident would raise nosy questions.

"How is the ankle?" Brooke asked. "Mum said you'd been out for three weeks so far."

"That bites," one of the rugby players said. "I had a groin injury last season and hated every day I was off the field."

Holly offered an understanding smile, totally in sync with his dislike of injuries. "The physio has cleared me for light training next week. He said I could play soon—in around two weeks. The injury has healed better than the doctor expected, which makes me lucky."

The rugby player nodded. "Fantastic news."

"Can I steal my roomie for a dance?" Angus's smooth voice cut through the discussions. He held out his hand, and Holly stood, placing her fingers in his. "Are you okay to dance with your ankle?"

"I think so, as long as we don't try any fast moves."

"We'll keep to a slow crawl," he promised.

A tiny shimmer of nerves skipped through her during their stroll to the dance floor. *Jeepers.* Jealous and nervous on the same night. This was Angus. Above all, he was her friend. He wouldn't hurt her.

She slipped into his arms, her heels making them almost the same height. His hands rested on her shoulders, the delicate brush of fingers sending a rash of goosebumps across her skin.

"The dinner hasn't been too distressing," she said as they moved in time to the music.

"I'd like it better if I could hold you closer." He ran his hands down her bare back and let them come to rest on her butt. There they hovered, branding her flesh beneath the silky gown. His brows rose. "Why, Ms. Blackwood, where are your panties?"

"In the drawer at home." Her chin lifted, and their gazes met, held. Sensual tension swept between them, choking the air, stealing her breath. "I thought you'd like that."

"This is thought-provoking information." His hands wandered across her buttocks.

"You get off on teasing me."

"Yes, I do. Right now, the temptation is to rush you off the dance floor, find a secluded spot, shove you against the nearest wall, and finger you until you scream my name." His chuckle sounded ragged at the edges. "And that's just for starters."

Holly swallowed, and her sex fluttered at the dark promise in his husky voice. "How much longer do we need to stay?"

"An hour at the most. Once the sponsors leave, we can head home."

"Okay." Holly didn't think she'd last that long, not with the delicate brush of his fingers on her bottom. Each touch zapped her with intense bursts of arousal, enticing her to fall into his arms and hang the consequences.

His mouth brushed her ear once the music ended. "I'll count the minutes while I plan what to do to you first."

"Angus, do you have a moment?" one of the management staff asked, coming up behind them as they drifted off the dance floor.

"Sure. I'll catch up with you soon," Angus said in a low voice. "Think of me."

As if she could do anything else when her body craved his cock and his skilled touch. She flexed her inner muscles, savored the quick whoosh of heat. *Oh, boy. Mind off, Angus.* Hurriedly, she tottered over to her chair and sat before her knees failed.

"So, how was the honeymoon?" she asked Brooke when her sister dropped into the empty seat beside Holly.

"Let's not talk about me. What's happening between you and Angus?"

"I told you before. We're friends." Holly forced her expression to neutral and stared at her sister while trying to feign puzzlement. "What?"

"I've known you since our parents reconnected and married. I can spot a lie when I see one."

Holly wrinkled her nose. "I should've kicked up a bigger fuss when my father decided to make an honest woman of his high school sweetheart."

Brooke snorted. "Enough of the family drama. I recognize snowballing when I hear it."

Holly clicked her fingers. "Damn." Her eyes narrowed. "You're a fine one to talk."

"Secrets," Brooke mused. "Secrets are interesting things."

"For goodness sake. You want the truth? I earn a pittance at the bank, and Tara has been a pain in my butt. I couldn't afford the apartment rent by myself and didn't know what to do."

"Mum and Dad would—"

"Damn it, I can't hit them up for another loan when I haven't paid off any of the first one. Angus offered a solution, and I took it."

"I saw the way you were looking at each other on the dance floor."

"Oh, that. A woman on the cheer squad is giving Angus a hard time. She won't take no for an answer. He asked me to help him out."

"Who?" Brooke demanded.

"Casey." Her sister was a tough nut, or maybe she knew Holly too well.

"*Huh*. Casey made a pass at Seb recently." Anger twisted her face from pretty to determined. "Someone needs to take that conniving hussy down."

"Angus didn't want to make a fuss."

"No, he wouldn't with management and sponsors present. Are you sure there's no hope of anything between you?"

"No spark."

Brooke sighed in disappointment. Holly thought she might say more, but Seb approached them.

He gave Holly a cool nod and turned to his wife. "Are you ready to go home?"

"Sure thing," Brooke said, standing. "I'll talk to you tomorrow."

Brooke and Seb strode away, Seb whispering something in her sister's ear that made her giggle. Brooke seemed happy, and Holly was glad. She hoped it lasted. If she caught Seb doing something wrong, she'd castrate him herself.

"Would you like to dance?" Adam, a lanky flanker for the Auckland Dragons, tapped her on the shoulder. He gave her a crooked grin, his blue eyes a tad bashful beneath his black brows and shaggy brown hair.

She searched out Angus and saw he was still busy discussing rugby with sponsors. "As long as you keep to the slow stuff. Can you dance?"

"I can, but those bozos over there don't believe me. Can you dance?"

"Afraid I'll show you up?" Adam was younger than her

by about two years but an upcoming star on the rugby field.

"Nope. It's a win-win for me. I get to dance with a pretty lady and to collect the bet from my mates." He held out his hand. "Let's make them eat their words."

Holly was breathless when she arrived back at the table, but she was pleased to note her ankle had survived the dancing and wasn't protesting one bit.

Adam kissed her on the cheek. "Thanks, Holly. I owe you."

"No problem." The prickling at her nape gave her a clue of Angus's return.

"Are you ready to leave?"

"I am. Thanks for the dance, Adam." And with a wave, she followed Angus from the function room.

Angus signaled a cab and ushered her inside when the vehicle pulled up next to them. He slid into the seat beside her, his hard thigh pressing against hers.

"Did you enjoy yourself?" His warm breath caressed her ear.

"More than I thought I would. Even the food was better than I expected. Normally the meat tastes as if it's a cousin to rubber. My lemon chicken was delicious."

"You enjoyed the dancing."

She turned her head to read his expression. It told her nothing, and she rushed into speech. "Adam is like a gamboling puppy. He's fun." *But he feels like a brother, unlike you.*

"He's a good kid." Angus picked up her hand and stroked the back.

"He's not a womanizer like some others," she replied.

By the time the cab pulled up outside the apartment, nervousness had a tight grip on her. Holly winged a glance at Angus as they entered the building. His expression didn't tell her anything. Together, they waited for the elevator. The doors opened, closed, and he reached for her, slamming his mouth on hers, bold and demanding. His kiss sent urgency coursing the length of her body. Pleasure. Yearning. The elevator reached their floor, and he grasped her hand, tugging her to his apartment.

"I want you," he said.

"Mutual," she whispered, taking in the glitter of passion and lust in his blue eyes.

In seconds flat, he'd opened the door and yanked her inside. He shoved her against the wall and claimed her mouth. Ravenous need poured from him into her, and she pressed close, rubbing her body sensually against his limbs.

Angus slid his hand beneath the hem of her red dress. "Thigh-high stockings. Nice," he murmured against her mouth. His fingers traced over the strip of bare skin above the lacy elastic holding them in place. Back and forth, back and forth until the intimate stroke drew dampness from her, coating her folds.

His hand journeyed higher and traced a delicate path

along her slit. She trembled and sagged against him, drawing in his scent and savoring his strength. He caressed her clit, giving her the merest pressure when she craved much more.

"Angus." His name was a protest. "No teasing."

"But I make you happy."

"That's true." She acted like putty at his slightest touch.

His busy hands stroked and teased, pushing her higher but not enough to come.

"Please."

"Please what?"

She winked at him. "Please, sir."

Angus rolled his eyes. "So irreverent. I wonder if you'll be as cheeky when I restrain you. Maybe tie you up with ropes."

The humor left her, replaced by dizzy eagerness. The spanking had made her hot—in more ways than she'd expected. The women's libber in her quailed at the idea of a man disciplining her. Her feminine side had enjoyed the unexpectedness of his smacks. Her tongue flicked out to moisten her bottom lip, her pulse jumping when she noticed his avid interest.

"I...I think I might like that."

"Jesus," he whispered, his thumb skating over her clit. He removed his hand and licked her juices from his fingers.

Angus stepped back and stripped off his jacket. He unfastened his belt and pulled it from his pants. The belt buckle clanked when it hit the floor beside his suit jacket. The zipper of his trousers sounded loud in the silence, almost as noisy as the pounding of her heart.

She watched each action, her blood racing and sinking into her lower body. A throb of need pumped in time with her heartbeat. The crinkle of a wrapper drew her brows together, but her forehead smoothed as she watched Angus pull his erection from his boxer-briefs and roll the condom into place.

Then, his gaze met hers, eyes heavy-lidded, and he pounced, pushing her against the wall, his hands darting under the hem of her dress. "Hands on my shoulders."

She obeyed instantly, having learned his way always brought extra pleasure. He spread her thighs with his knee and guided his cock up and down her slit. She craved more pressure, and her hips rose upward in silent demand. Angus laughed and crushed his mouth against hers, tasting and nipping her lip before soothing it with a firm lick.

She felt him penetrate her, pushing inside her clinging pussy while his finger played her clit. Holly buried her face against his neck, breathing in his aftershave and his underlying spicy scent.

"God, you're incredible," he murmured. "Hold on to my shoulders and wrap your legs around my hips."

A hungry little noise escaped her as he increased the pressure against her swollen bud. He shafted her deeply, filling her, invading, retreating, teasing.

"You close?" He rasped out the demand.

"Yes." Even as she answered, the walls of her sex pulsated, and hot desire streaked along her legs to her toes. It consumed her, her orgasm stealing her thoughts and tossing her into a sea of pleasure. Overload. So good she wanted a repeat, just as soon as she strung together the request.

He let out a murmur of satisfaction, hastened his thrusts, his cock hammering into her, raw male desire twisting his features. He stilled, embedded deep inside her, his strangled moan telling of his enjoyment.

When her brain rebooted, she released her grip on his hips and balanced on trembling legs.

He caressed her face, his eyes smoldering with passion. "I needed that."

Holly glanced at her crumpled dress. "We're both still dressed."

"And soon we won't be." He righted his trousers and scooped her off her feet. "Might as well save you the extra walking. We don't want to test your ankle too much."

A girlie *eek* escaped, and Holly clutched his shoulders. "I'm capable of walking. Your coaches will have my head if you hurt your back."

"I want to lug you about."

"Oh, if you put it that way." She snuggled against him, the novelty of him caring for her turning her insides to mush. The man was spoiling her with his generous loving and the ease in which their lives had combined. He never expected her to do the chores and did his fair share whenever he was around.

He set her on the bed and kneeled to unfasten her shoes. Gentle hands rolled her stockings down her legs.

"Turn around and let me get the back."

He made quick work of undressing her, leaving her quivering and needy. She cocked her head, studying him as he stripped. "Are you going to tie me up?"

"Not tonight," he said, reaching into a drawer. "But I will use these."

Holly stared at the set of handcuffs dangling from his finger. "You will not use those on me." The words burst from her, even though he'd already mentioned restraints.

"Is that a dare? You should know better."

"What if there's a fire and I'm cuffed to the bed," she said, frowning at the bed frame.

Angus wanted to laugh. Instead, he kept his face impassive and waited for a beat for her to decide if the handcuffs were acceptable. "You didn't seem to mind the idea of ropes."

"You weren't kidding?"

"Was I telling the truth about the spanking?"

"Yes."

"I like to get adventurous in bed, Holly, but I'd never go too far and injure you. We do this safely. You get to say no anytime you want. If things become too intense, all you need to do is say no or better yet, let's give you a safe word. How about netball? If you mention netball, I'll release you immediately." When she didn't reply, he reached for her nearest hand and clicked one padded cuff around her wrist.

"Tell me this is okay. I want to hear your consent before I continue."

She studied him closely. "If I say netball, you'll release me immediately?"

"I promise. I'll also put the keys under your pillow. There will be enough slack for you to unlock the cuffs if you want."

Holly cocked her head a fraction, then nodded. "All right. I agree to this."

Gratitude and excitement filled him as he leaned over her torso. He inhaled her orange blossom perfume and stole a kiss. He lifted one hand above her head and attached the cuff to the frame of the bed. With a reassuring smile, he shut that one too, and the chain rattled.

The atmosphere in the room thickened. She blew out her breath, her eyes huge and staring right at him.

"Don't look so nervous." Angus let his eyes roam her naked body, his to play with, to touch, and fuck. His grin widened at the blush stealing over her cheeks. "I want to make you feel extra good."

She licked her lips and shifted her weight, making the cuffs clack against the iron of the headboard. "That's what worries me. What's next?"

"That's for me to know and you to find out." He ran his hand along her arm, noting the ripple of chill bumps pebbling her skin. "You have pretty breasts."

"I wish you'd do more than stare."

A chuckle pushed past his guard. "Patience, my little chickadee." He laughed at her wrinkled nose and wondered what other endearments he could try. Angus slid off the bed and opened the bottom drawer of the nightstand. His hand hovered over his selection of toys, and he chose a vibrator and a set of nipple clamps.

He returned and set the toys by his side. She lay like a treasure spread out in front of him, and impatience grabbed him in a ruthless grip. Unable to delay a millisecond longer, he trailed his fingers down the middle of her chest.

"Is that all you're going to do? Torture me?"

He cupped one breast and tested the weight before lowering his head to taste her. With his tongue, he sucked and worried her nipple until it turned a dark pink. "That's a lovely sight."

Angus picked up one clamp and attached it to her nipple. Holly made a hissing sound, her eyes still big and wide as she watched him. He turned his attention to her other breast, taking pleasure in the soft cries he drew from her. It was a fine thing, watching her eyes darken and go almost blank. He clipped on the second clamp and attached a delicate silver chain to connect the two. A gentle tug on the chain drew a ragged gasp from her. She lifted her hips, and when he gave the chain a second flick, a moan rolled up her throat.

"Gorgeous," he said, moving lower. "Part your legs for me. No, a fraction wider. Perfect. I want to see your pretty pussy."

"I'd prefer you inside me."

"Good things come to those who wait."

"I've never liked that quote. My father used to say it all the time. *Ugh*. Now you've made me think of my father and sex in the same sentence." She shuddered theatrically. "That's plain wrong."

Delighted with her, he grinned and dipped his head to sample her juices. He nuzzled her clit with his chin first, then drew his tongue along her folds. She lifted into his touch, trying to deepen the contact. Instead, he kept it light, wanting to tease her first, make her desperate for release. He delved with his tongue, licked, and pushed her craving to higher levels.

"Angus," she whispered, her thighs tense beneath his touch.

He reached up to pull the chain connecting the clamps while he circled her swollen clit, working her closer to orgasm. A rough, punishing lick made her jerk. He thrust his tongue past her entrance, tasting her scorching arousal.

Damn. The urge to shove his dick in her pulled at him,

the rich rush of desire disintegrating his willpower and pushing him into a raw place of need. His balls drew up, tight and painful, and he had to shake his head to get his mind back on Holly.

He grabbed the vibrator and pushed it inside her, switching it on but keeping the speed low.

"Damn, Angus. You're torturing me here."

"Not torture, lovely. I aim to make you feel very, very good." He crawled up her body and took her mouth while playing with the chain attached to the clamps. The hunger inside him poured past his lips, flowed into her and ricocheted back with an arrow of heat.

His cock ached, pre-come giving a shine to the head. Bugger this. He reached down and turned up the vibrator.

"Ugh," Holly protested. "Angus, don't tease me." Her arms jerked against the cuffs, straining to touch as he was touching her. He played her body, controlling the lift of her hips, and enjoyed the hell out of her pleas. He tugged on the chain and caught the flare of desire in her.

"Look at you," he whispered, awed by the carnal hunger shimmering in her eyes. He intended to travel to those places with her. He kept kissing her as if he could never get enough of her. Heady stuff. When he lifted his lips, he didn't dally, maintaining the vibrator speed—hard enough to keep her on edge yet not enough to throw her into the waiting sensual turmoil.

He trailed his fingers down her neck, using light pressure

and making her aware of his power. But instead of frightening her, his domineering manner pushed her harder, bringing a delicate flush to her skin. He kissed along her throat and nipped.

Her eyes darkened. "Angus."

"I want to fuck you so bad. Come for me so I can."

"Together," she said.

"You first." His tone brooked no argument, and he reached lower to push the vibrator controls to a high setting.

The vibrations annihilated the last of the strings holding her earthbound. Pleasure burst upon her, so fine it verged on pain. Holly gasped, her sex clenching around the vibrator in hard, quick spasms.

Her sound of excitement, the way she shuddered, seemed to act as his signal. Angus yanked the humming sex toy from her. Seconds later and suited up, he thrust into her quivering flesh.

With each plunge, the friction of his chest moved the chain attaching the nipple clamps. Tiny spikes of pleasure-pain leaped from her breasts, reverberating throughout her entire body. The sweet agony increased, and she exploded in another orgasm, panting to get her breath while the pleasure dragged her under into a place where sensation ruled.

Angus didn't mess around. He drove into her, pushing

her up the mattress with the force of his thrusts. Fast. Rough, and she loved every moment. She stared up at his rugged visage, the savageness in his expression, and gloried in seeing him like this.

A guttural groan burst from him, and he stilled, his chest rising and falling at a rapid pace, his eyes squeezed tightly shut.

She'd kept hers open the entire time.

His eyes popped open, and Holly gaped at the passion and the chase of his emotions. They were too quick for her to read with accuracy. He leaned over and brushed an unhurried kiss on her lips. A tender kiss. Loving, even. "You okay?"

Holly nodded, unsure of what to say. This—whatever it was between them—fell into a different category than friends, which confused her. *He* confused her.

"Excellent." Angus pulled out of her and removed the condom with a snap. A smile wreathed his lips when he returned and stopped by the bed to study her. He leaned closer, and she caught a whiff of his spicy aftershave and their shared passion. He tucked a strand of hair behind her ear. "I usually enjoy our away games and staying in a hotel with the rest of the team, but it was weird not waking up with you in my bed."

"I missed you too." Nothing less than the truth.

He sat beside her, his fingers gentle against her breasts, and removed the chain connecting the clamps. "This will hurt when I release the clips. It's the blood rushing back."

"Okay." Even she heard her doubt.

"Take a deep breath," he ordered. "Once I take the clamp off, let your breath ease out slowly."

He hadn't steered her wrong yet, so she obeyed, sucking in a quick draft of air. He unclipped one clamp. "Ouch," she spat. "That hurts."

"Shush, let me make it better." He leaned over and surrounded her aching tip with his wet mouth. Instead of the hard suction she'd expected, this time, he licked and kept his attentions gentle. The hard pulse from the rush of blood receded and faded.

He repeated the move on her other nipple, and this time she was prepared for the sharp bite. She breathed through the pain, almost sighing with pleasure when his mouth surrounded her nipple, the caress of his tongue soothing the residual ache from the clamp.

She shifted, her shoulders protesting the unnatural position.

Angus burrowed under the pillow to retrieve the key. He unlocked the cuffs, released her wrists, and massaged her shoulders. "Turn over for me, blossom." He helped her reposition, and she heard the slide of a drawer opening.

The scent of lavender floated into her senses, and she sighed. Although an old-fashioned fragrance, she liked it. Soon his hands slid over her shoulders, massaging away the aches and stiffness.

"You're good at that," she murmured, so relaxed she thought she might fall off to sleep.

"I asked the team medical staff to give me lessons," Angus said. "I figured it was a handy skill to acquire."

"Well, you're talented at it." She tried not to think of the other women on whom he'd practiced his skills. *Stupid, don't steer your thoughts in that direction.* "What happens if I get too comfortable with our relationship?"

"There's nothing wrong with contentment." His hands had stilled for an instant, but he resumed his stroking and began digging into her muscles and sliding his palms across her heated skin. "I don't want dramatics and constant bickering. No man does. We're simple creatures and prefer harmony, clean socks, and pressed shirts."

A laugh bubbled out of her. "I might call you sir on occasion, but there is no way in hell I'm gonna start ironing your shirts."

"I'm certain I'd do a better job anyway," he said. "My mother taught me how to press my garments."

He didn't mention his family much, but whenever he did, his voice held genuine affection. Good to know.

His hands slid lower to knead her buttocks, diverting her attention. "That feels decadent."

He parted her legs, and she let him direct her position, too maxed out on bliss to argue about him gawking at her butt. He'd studied and touched her all over, anyway. His skilled hands wandered lower to the place where her backside ended and her legs began. A tremor stirred in her belly—a prickle of pleasant warmth she recognized as sexual. Angus excelled at this stuff, playing her like an instrument.

Strong fingers slid along her inner thighs while he massaged her upper legs. Silently she begged him to detour, but he added more oil and worked his magic on her calves, her feet, avoiding her injured ankle to push on pressure points.

Holly sank deeper into the mattress, relaxed yet still aware of every touch.

"Turn over for me."

She flopped over, her gaze seeking him out.

"Close your eyes. Relax, darlin'."

"Open your eyes. Shut your eyes. You need to make your mind up, buddy."

"I'll stop." His words weren't a threat, but she knew he meant them.

She closed her eyes, a hint of lavender swirled around her, and his hands made contact with her breasts. Her nipples were still tender from the clamps, but he was gentle, his touch soothing. Holly drifted again, her mind flitting but not settling on a particular topic. Instead, she focused on the magical way he made her muscles sing with pleasure.

"Splay your legs again," he said. "I need to sit between them."

Silently, she complied, too relaxed now to force her eyes open. His hands drifted over her hips and skipped to her thighs with long feathering strokes. The slight pressure against her muscles loosened them before he moved downward. He worked on her ankle, using delicate brushes of his fingers, and paid attention to her toes.

Finally, his hands lifted. Her body hummed, yet contrarily her muscles were so relaxed she doubted her limbs would hold her upright. A click sounded—the recapping of a bottle. The mattress shifted when he moved, but still, she didn't open her eyes.

A wet heat slid the length of her folds, a warmth surrounded her clit, and slight suction sent her body soaring. Oh, god. Damn, he was excellent at keeping her off-balance. Her orgasm was quick and rolled over her like a gentle wave, leaving her boneless.

The mattress shifted again, and a gentle kiss landed on her lips. A blanket landed on top of her.

"Sleep," he whispered.

Inside, Holly chuckled, but part of her cried too, and fatigue pulled at her. Angus had given her a happy ending. He wanted nothing more than friendship, and he'd confirmed this from the beginning. This...thing...between them was convenient. That's all. She must protect her heart because at some time during the past weeks, she'd lost her bias against rugby player boyfriends.

9

New Beginnings and Temptations

"I start my new job today," Holly said on Monday morning. She accepted the coffee Angus handed her with a smile of thanks and inhaled the decadent aroma. The radio played in the background, a woman reading out the morning's headlines, but her attention fixed on Angus.

"Scared?" Angus's cocky grin had her heart beating faster. He pressed a kiss to her cheek before pulling back to snag two slices of toast from the toaster. "Holly?"

"Oh!" She struggled to get her head back in the game. "A little. I'm going to be naughty." She swallowed a mouthful of coffee and slid onto a barstool at the breakfast counter. "Last week, the doctor gave me an additional medical certificate through to the end of this week. I'm handing in my notice at the bank today and pretending I need the rest of the days off sick."

"You only need to give a week's notice?"

"Ideally, we should give two weeks, but I'm a part-timer, and my contract specifies a week. Tara can't make me give two weeks notice."

"Good luck."

Holly fixed her lips in a smile and admitted that she wasn't eager for a Tara confrontation despite her bravado. "This time, I have the cards in my hand."

The new job was a breeze. She sat at a desk, which kept the weight off her ankle and answered calls from bank customers. A manual helped her with the answers she didn't know, but her previous knowledge of bank workings held her in good stead. Judy, the woman assigned to help her, moved back to her desk after a nod of approval.

"How did the new job go?" Angus asked when she arrived home that night from a light training run.

"Great. The other people in the call center are friendly. I like my boss, and my coworkers have already invited me out to drinks on Thursday night."

"And Tara?"

"Was her usual bitchy self. I surprised her today. After she reamed me for taking so much time off work, I handed in my notice." Anger pumped through Holly when she recalled the scene. "She threatened to withhold a reference. Not that the bank references are stellar. They issue a certificate showing the length of service, and that's it. Policy."

"Didn't the call center ring her for a reference?"

"No. I told them Tara and I had a personality conflict. Instead, I provided them with heaps of character references, and it helped that Susan, the woman who interviewed me, is a netball fan. She recognized me."

"Lucky break."

"It was. Do you have an away game this weekend?"

"Yes, we're off to Canberra."

"I'll be in Australia too. Sydney, but not until Sunday."

A grin spread across his face. "You're playing?"

"There's a possibility I might go on for the last five minutes of the game in the wing defense position. My ankle held up during the brief training run, and the coach wants me to test it."

"How come you're on the wing?"

Holly scrunched up her nose. "Less jumping. Less pressure on my ankle. We're also short in that position. The coach suspended Karen for unbecoming behavior."

"What does that mean?"

"Evidently, she was the one who pushed me. I don't know what the fuss is about since I'm positive it was an accident." Except there had been that weird conversation... "Did you date Karen?"

Angus winced. "Not my finest moment. We didn't mesh, but I can't see your teammate trying to hurt you.

That makes little sense."

"That's what I've been telling everyone. If she swung that way, surely she'd go after Carly. She's always raving about you."

Angus took on a pained expression. "How is your ankle, truly?"

"Not a twinge." Holly let him change the subject. "The physio said I've healed better than he expected. I guess those extra sick days I took helped. I'm going to keep resting my ankle as much as possible, though. Baby it for as long as I can. When do you fly out?"

"Friday. We have a light training session on Thursday."

Holly nodded, wanting to invite Angus along to drinks—her new friends had said it was very casual and she could bring a boyfriend if she wanted. Holly had told them she didn't have a boyfriend, which was technically correct, so why did guilt fill her now?

"Something wrong?"

She shook herself. "No, everything is fine. I didn't sleep well last night. Guess today stressed me more than I thought it would."

Angus walked over to her and slid an arm around her shoulders. He gave her a quick hug. "You've had lots to worry about recently. Want to watch a movie after dinner? I made soup and grabbed a loaf of fancy bread from the bakery on the way home from training today."

"Sounds great. You know, if your fans realized big rugby

stars don't go out on the town every night, it might shock them."

"I don't need alcohol and publicity to boost my ego." His tone was noticeably cooler.

"No, you don't. You're perfect the way you are, and I'm happy to reap the benefits of your ability in the kitchen."

His gaze narrowed, his expression one she was beginning to recognize. His sex face. "I haven't shown you all my kitchen skills."

She held up her hands in a back-off signal. "Oh, no, you don't. You promised me food and a movie. I'm too tired for seduction."

"But that's the thing about seduction, darling Holly. You don't have to do anything except succumb."

She found herself trapped between the kitchen counter and his muscular torso, her own body on immediate high alert. His mouth crushed hers, and with a groan, she surrendered. An instant later, he swung her into his arms and placed her on the sofa.

Her clothes disappeared at speed, his vanquished to a heap on the floor. He sucked low on her neck, leading her into temptation.

"Angus." She stepped into the fire and passion, groaning with pleasure when he slipped between her legs, pinning her with his strength and his cock. "Yes."

He thrust hard and fast, the friction between their bodies so good it was almost unbearable. She scaled the peaks, her gaze on his face, his intense expression. A moan escaped as she held him tight against her body, quaking with desperate need, desperate hunger.

"Come for me, sweet pea."

The overpowering sensations became too much. She gulped in air and toppled into soul-deep pleasure. She watched Angus's face contort, and his hips bucked as he pounded into her and finally stilled.

Long moments later, he lapped at the perspiration coating her skin, murmured soft words she couldn't hear. She moaned a protest when he withdrew and shifted his weight.

"How about dinner in the bedroom?" he asked. "It'll be warmer in there." Without waiting for her answer, he scooped her up again and carried her to the master bedroom. She crawled into bed, closed her eyes, and dropped into an exhausted sleep.

ON THURSDAY NIGHT, HOLLY dropped by the pub with her workmates. Other people, straight from work, packed the Irish-theme pub. Holly took in the dark wood paneling and the collection of musical instruments hanging on the walls. The background music flowed through her body and made her feet itch to dance. Instead, she followed her new friends straight to the far corner. Miraculously, they found a long table with three lone inhabitants and took immediate possession.

"I'll get you a drink. What would you like?"

Daniel, Holly recalled after a brief dig in her memory. She smiled and shook her head. "Thanks, but I'm on a budget. I can't afford to reciprocate." Easier to be upfront from the start.

"Just one drink," he said in a coaxing tone. "No expectations, I promise."

"Thanks," Holly said finally. "A glass of house sav blanc, please."

Daniel strode away, and Holly watched him until he disappeared into the throng of customers circling the bar. Tall with a cute blond surfer-boy attitude, he seemed popular with everyone at work. She'd noticed he didn't flirt, but he possessed a healthy slice of charm that he used to good effect.

"Daniel likes you." Judy, her trainer, bore a broad smile, and it lit up her freckled face.

Caution made Holly ask. "Is that a problem?"

Judy smoothed a lock of red hair behind her ear. "No, of course not. Daniel is great, but normally we're a friends-only group. No romantic tangles anywhere. This is a first for Daniel."

"He seems...nice." Holly felt the heat crawl up her throat. Daniel was more than agreeable. He was an attractive specimen, and a woman would need to be deaf and blind to miss his appeal.

"Daniel is great. You don't need to worry. You're not stepping on anyone's toes. As far as I know, he broke up with his girlfriend last month."

"Oh." What the heck was she doing? Angus... Holly's thoughts drifted as she tried to squelch her guilt and the misgivings that jumped out to seize her by the throat.

"One glass of wine," Daniel said, offering her the glass.

"Thanks." Holly slid along the bench seat to give him a space. Just good manners. She wasn't doing anything wrong.

The group chatted, drawing Holly in and making her feel welcome. The conversation ranged over myriad topics, and Holly listened and watched the dynamics. This new job was a lucky break. With the work pressure resolved, she could concentrate on getting back on the starting team.

"When's your next game, Holly?" Judy asked.

"I'm hoping I get a little court time on Sunday."

The girls started talking netball, and it turned out there were several fans.

"Let us know about your next home game," Judy said. "We'll be your cheering squad. Our bank sponsors the team, so we should score enough tickets."

The guys turned the talk to rugby and the upcoming game for the Auckland team.

"Do you follow rugby?" Daniel asked, pulling her into the conversation.

"Sure. My roomie plays for the Dragons, and my sister is on the cheer squad. I know quite a few of the guys on the team."

The table turned silent as everyone stared at her.

"My God," Judy said, holding her hands over her heart and pretending awe. "We're sitting with sports royalty."

Holly made a rude sound that vibrated past her lips, then wrinkled her nose to punctuate her feelings. Everyone grinned.

"Who's your roomie?" Daniel asked.

"Angus O'Neil."

"You share a flat with Angus O'Neil!" one girl screeched. "Be still, my heart." She leaned closer, her brown eyes full of nosy intent. "Tell me you've seen his naked butt."

A blast of fierce heat flooded Holly's cheeks, and she thought of a pithy curse, her thoughts pedaling madly while she attempted to fashion a reply. Aware everyone was waiting, judging, jumping to conclusions, she decided on a partial truth. "We share an apartment. That's all."

"Why are you blushing?" the girl asked again, her eyes doing a visual version of a slice and dice.

"It's hot in here," she said.

"Nah, you've seen his butt," someone else said, amusement coloring his tone.

"A clothed one." Holly sighed and lied through her teeth. "More's the pity. But I have a fertile imagination."

"Is he dating anyone?" a girl with long brunette hair

asked. "The gossip magazines always show him with so many different women."

"Not that I know of. His rugby commitments keep him busy. He's away a lot, and I hardly see him. I'm away most weekends too, which makes sharing an apartment perfect. It's like I have my own place."

"I'm jealous," the brunette said. "I have to share a place with three others—just to afford the rent. Auckland is so expensive."

"Tell me about it. I used to share with my sister, but the rent on my own—impossible," Holly said.

"So, how did you end up sharing with Angus?" Daniel asked.

"Good timing," Holly said. "We met at a party, and he mentioned he needed someone to house-sit while he was away. It's worked out well."

"Do we get an invitation to visit?" Judy asked.

"No way," Holly said, laughing to take the sting out of her words. "You just want to paw through Angus's underwear."

Judy blasted her with a grin and clicked her fingers. "Damn. Busted."

To Holly's relief, talk drifted away from her sexy roomie. She caught snatches of conversation about work, about the lawyers in the opposite building, car repairs, and the cost of a flight to Sydney.

Holly took a sip of her wine, tossed a comment into the

conversation now and then, but mostly listened.

"You're going to be very popular around here," Daniel murmured.

"Why?"

"You're in with the sports world."

"And I thought it was my pretty face," Holly said.

"That too." Daniel glanced up and down the table and turned back to focus on her. "Would you like to go out with me? We could see a movie or have dinner?"

Holly's heart hammered, and she felt a fierce need to lick her lips. "When?" It was the only word she managed. Her mind was screaming at her to tell him no, but how could she when she'd denied an intimate relationship with Angus five minutes ago? Heat flushed her face and crawled down her neck. She rubbed a tight spot on her chest while telling herself this was wrong.

"Tomorrow night?"

"That would work, as long as we're not too late. I have a training run on Saturday morning." What was she doing? Self-protection, her heart told her. She and Angus... She cut off her thoughts and tried to concentrate on the present.

"We'll go to an early session," Daniel said, obvious pleasure sparkling through him at her acquiescence. "I'll make sure you're home at a reasonable hour. We can go straight from work."

"Okay." Holly managed a shaky smile and sipped more

of her wine. What she had with Angus wouldn't last anyway, not given her record. He'd soon lose interest and want to move on, and she accepted that. Perhaps it was better if she made the initial break. Besides, Daniel seemed nice, and he wasn't involved in rugby. A definite plus.

"Do you spend a lot of hours training?" he asked.

Back on familiar ground, she answered without hesitation, not having to censor her words. "I have to work hard for a chance of making the national team."

"That's the goal?"

"I've wanted to pull on the black uniform ever since I was a kid. Now all I have to do is make it happen."

"They say drive and determination are half the battle, and it's obvious you have those," Daniel said. "When do you play next at home?"

"We have a game in Hamilton next weekend," Holly said. "We're playing a New Zealand team—the Diamonds."

"You're not in the top four teams on the table, though," another of the girls said, joining the conversation.

"No, we're about sixth. I don't think we'll make the top four—not unless we win the rest of our games. The competition is tough this year."

"Who's for another drink?" one of the guys said.

"Holly?" Daniel asked.

Holly shook her head. "I'd better not. I need to get up for a run early tomorrow morning." She checked her watch.

"I'd better get going if I want to squeeze in a gym session tonight."

"Wow, the training would kill me," Judy said. "You have dedication."

"You like your social life too much," Daniel teased.

"Too right," Judy agreed. "You're only young once."

"How are you getting home?" Daniel asked.

"Walk. The apartment is ten minutes from here."

"You're not walking on your own," Judy protested. "It's dark out there."

"I'm always careful," Holly said. "I'll be fine."

Daniel stood. "I'll walk you."

"You don't have to." Holly stood and called a general goodbye. She pulled on her gray winter coat—a gift from Brooke—and buttoned it against the cool night air.

"I want to," he said, grasping her hand in his in a no-nonsense manner. "Come on."

"You coming back, Daniel?" one guy asked. "I was going to offer you a lift home."

Daniel nodded. "I'll be back for you to shout me a drink."

Everyone hooted, and there was a great chorus of goodbyes. Holly's heart thumped a little faster as Daniel tugged her through the crowd in the pub. He protected her from pushing and shoving with his larger frame and cleared the way to the door. His hand was warm and comforting and given time, she suspected she'd come to like this man. He had a calm vibe, and it was apparent he was popular with his peers.

If only Angus didn't stand in the way.

And her guilty conscience.

"Which way?" Daniel asked when they stepped into the night. The earlier rain had stopped, leaving the footpaths wet. A sullen moon played peek-a-boo with the clouds, and a sea breeze blew off the harbor, slapping her cheeks with an icy chill.

"It's cold out here. There's no need for you to freeze as well."

"Stop arguing," he said, displaying clear determination.

Holly gave up and gestured to the left. "This way." She skirted a puddle and started walking. Daniel fell into step.

"What sort of movies do you like?"

"Chick flicks," she said, biting the inside of her cheek.

"Oh," he said. "I guess we can watch one of those."

Her laughter rang out as they reached the water and headed for the bridge crossing the marina. "Sucked in," she said. "That was effortless."

"You don't like chick flick movies?"

"I don't mind what we watch. I love movies and watch all types."

"Good," he said with relief. "I was trying to make a good impression and was willing to compromise."

Her heart fluttered his admission. "I'm pretty easygoing." Too laidback and accepting, according to

Brooke. She let men walk over her, except she hadn't with Angus. Or at least their relationship differed from her previous ones. Yes, she let him guide her sexually, but she made her own decisions out of the bedroom.

"Okay, we'll head out straight after work and pick a movie together. Whatever works with our schedule to get you an early night."

"Deal," she said.

"What do you do in your spare time?" he asked.

She laughed. "Leisure hours, you mean? During the netball season, my life is full of training and games. When I'm not playing, I'm watching games and learning. I practice my ball skills and keep in shape. I fit in sleeping or resting in between."

"And during the summer?"

"I increase my work hours and try to find a second job. Netball cuts into the hours I can work during the season."

"That's a lot of sacrifices."

"I'm driven." She wondered if he understood. "This is me here." She came to a halt at the apartment entrance and turned to him with a smile. In the light glowing from the door, she caught his expression and knew he wanted to kiss her. Stirrings of panic roared to life in her. *Act. Act now.*

She leaned closer and brushed a kiss on his cheek. "Thanks for walking me home."

"No problem." He stuffed his hands in the jacket pockets. "I'll see you tomorrow at work."

Behind them, a car slowed, and the roller door into the apartment garages rose.

"Tomorrow," she said, and with a final wave, she headed for the apartment entrance and punched in the code. After closing the door behind her, she stomped up the stairs.

The apartment was dark when she arrived, but a casserole filled the air with herbs and meaty goodness. Angus must have put on the slow cooker before he left for rugby practice. She dropped her bag in her room and shrugged out of her coat. Her belly gurgled with hunger, tempting her to ditch the gym session and eat instead.

Sighing, she unbuttoned her shirt and reached for a T-shirt. It was time for half an hour of light weights and stretches. Letting her fitness slide too much ranked as stupidity—just half an hour.

"Hi, honey. I'm home."

"Honey?" she asked, and he followed her voice and appeared in the doorway. "Really?"

"Your hair is the color of honey." He stepped inside the bedroom to snag her forearm and draw her against him. His scent was familiar and underscored with the tang of male sweat. She pressed her nose to his throat and drew in a second drag because the first one had smelled so enticing.

"Didn't you have time to shower?" Unease crept into her as she realized the car she'd heard enter the garage had belonged to Angus. Had he seen her kiss Daniel? Sure, the exchange hadn't reeked of passion, but she'd considered what being with Daniel would mean. Her mind had cheated or at least flirted with deepening a relationship with a man other than Angus.

"I thought I'd grab a shower at home. There's plenty of hot water, and I can watch you instead of hairy men. I might even entice you to shower with me."

"Not now. I'm going to the gym for half an hour."

"You don't want to overdo things," he warned.

Her temper flared. "I know what I need."

"I'll come with you."

"You don't need to babysit me. I won't overdo it—light weights and stretching. That's all." Holly dropped onto the bed to lace her shoes. "I'll see you later."

His jaw turned rigid, and irritation flashed in his eyes, but it disappeared so fast, she wasn't even sure of his mood. His tense jaw made her suspect he *had* seen her with Daniel, and she glanced away from him with a grimace.

"Have you had dinner?"

"No." A man didn't offer to serve dinner if he was that pissed. Right?

"The stew should be ready. I'll put on some potatoes. How does mash sound?"

"Fine." She turned away, but shame made her pause and reach for her manners. "Thanks."

Angus stared after her, his gut bucking with alarm. The urge to shake her and demand why she was doing this ate at him. He forced himself to remain still and breathe. In. Out. In. Out. He gripped the edge of the counter, the blood leaching from his knuckles while the savory stew aroma filled his lungs.

He'd seen her kiss the guy on the cheek and had thought nothing of it until she'd started behaving weirdly. Instinct told him to go after her, to request answers. He took half a step and reconsidered. No, he'd wait, allow her to confess.

In his bedroom, he stripped and naked, he strode into the en suite. Hell, of all the times to be flying out of the country. Where the hell had she met this dude? Work—it had to be at her new job.

After cleaning up and dressing in casual clothes, he kept busy with meal preparations. He speared a piece of steak and blew on it to cool the morsel before popping it into his mouth. It was cooked perfectly. He turned his attention to the potatoes.

Holly returned from the basement gym as Angus used a fork to test the readiness of the potatoes.

"How long do I have before dinner is ready?" she asked.

"Ten minutes," he said, adjusting his timing to allow for her shower.

With a nod, she turned away and disappeared.

Angus put his frustration into mashing the potatoes. The metallic thud of his masher against the pot interior rang out—*bang, thud, ding*. He'd spelled things out at the start. If she wanted out of their arrangement, all she had to do was ask. But fuck—he didn't want this to end.

In the distance, the shower turned off. He pulled heated plates from the oven, drained the peas he'd put on to heat—a last moment decision—and set two places at the breakfast bar.

Holly walked into the kitchen. "Can I do anything?"

"I've taken out a bottle of red wine. Will you pour?"

"Sure. How did your practice go?"

With his back to her, Angus mouthed a quick prayer of thanks. At least she'd recovered her temper and was striving for friendly. He could do affable as long as he discovered the truth at the same time. "Training was great. We worked on a few of our set moves. Nothing too strenuous. How was work?"

"I like the job and the other workers. We went out for drinks after closing."

With the guy on your own? Angus served up the meals and placed the plates on the woven mats.

"They're friendly and, from the sounds of it, go out together a lot. There were about twelve of us." She met his gaze without guilt, yet still, his gut twisted.

Fuck, enough of bloody pussyfooting around. "Was that you out front when I arrived home?"

"One of the guys walked me home." Holly glanced away, ostensibly to seat herself at the counter.

Despite her casual words, his unease increased. "That was gentlemanly of him."

"He insisted. I tried to tell him it's safe around here. He refused to take no for an answer."

"How's the ankle holding up? Are you running tomorrow morning?" Angus changed the subject because she wasn't giving him the answers he wanted, and he didn't want to fight. Not again.

"Yeah, I thought I'd go for a quick run."

"Good, I'll come with you. I don't need to leave for the airport until ten."

They ate their dinner, yet their ease with each other had disappeared. Instead, an elephant the size of a rugby field crouched in the middle of the room, and Holly seemed content to ignore its presence.

The phone buzzed, and Holly answered the call. She listened, then handed it over. "It's for you."

"O'Neil," he barked.

"Angus, it's Carly. I wondered if you were free on Saturday. I have a birthday party and would love to take you as my date."

"I have an away game."

"Oh, another time then," Carly said.

"I told you I don't have time for dating," Angus said. "Good night."

The phone rang again a beat later, and Angus picked it up, his scowl digging deep. "Hello," he barked before pausing for a second. "No, I'll be away. No, don't do that. Find someone else." He hung up.

The phone signaled another call. "What?" Angus snarled, then he relaxed on recognizing his cousin's wife. "Oh, sorry, Maggie. Sure, I'd love that. Can I bring a friend?" His gaze slid to Holly, who'd angled her body away from him. He caught her wrinkled brow, the way her arms wrapped around her middle. "Dinner sounds great."

Holly stood and went to make tea, obviously unwilling to listen any longer. When she returned, Angus stopped working on his tablet and battled his temper. Didn't she get that they were perfect together, and she was the only woman he wanted?

"You're getting a lot of calls lately," Holly said in an opening salvo.

"And I keep telling them I'm not interested." Despite his growing irritation, Angus kept his frustration and mouth buttoned. All he'd seen was a brief kiss—one kiss and nothing else to warrant his mind traveling toward betrayal. "That last call was Maggie, my cousin, Connor's wife. She wants us to go to dinner with them."

"Oh. Okay. That sounds lovely. Man, I'm beat." Holly thrust her hands in her pockets and shifted from foot to foot. "I'll help clean up and go to bed."

"There isn't much to do. I'll do the dishes."

"You sure?"

"No problem." His hands tightened on the plate he held, his knuckles turning white. He waited until Holly left the room before muttering a succinct curse. No way was he leaving the country with this tension between them. He stacked the dishwasher and put away the leftovers, his mind twisting and turning as he fashioned a plan.

When he stalked into his bedroom, Holly was already in bed and had left the lamp on for him. Some of his tension slipped away. She'd come to his bed instead of the room where she kept most of her possessions. He cleaned his teeth, stripped, and slid in beside her. He moved across the bed, the last of his apprehension fading when she wrapped her arms around him.

Their mouths met in a mutual explosion of hunger, her breasts enticingly brushing against his chest. He smoothed her hair away from her face and kissed down her body. "I want to taste you, feel you come against my mouth."

She gave a soft cry and arranged her body for his ease of access. Her fingers threaded through his hair and tugged, the sharp pain roaring straight to his cock.

"Hands above your head," he ordered. "Don't touch me until I tell you to move your hands."

"Bossy much?"

"Always," he grated out. "I want you wet before you touch me. I'm gonna finger you and make you come at least twice first."

A shudder passed through her. "Promises, promises."

"And then I'm going to put my cock inside your smart mouth to keep you busy."

"I'd enjoy that."

"I know I will." He licked and nibbled on her flesh, guided by her moans and cries. "You're so wet for me, angel. Always wet for me. Do you know how that makes me feel?"

"Lucky?" Part of her reply was a needy groan, her breathing harsh.

Angus lapped at her, plied her clit with his tongue, driving her deeper into lust and urgency. He thrust a finger inside her, worked her channel, and crooked his finger to stroke her sweet spot. For two strokes of his finger, she trembled, and then she cried out, her clit pulsing hard against his tongue.

"Again," he ordered, and he started teasing her, sliding two fingers inside her now while he sucked her clit, building up the sensual tension. With one hand, he reached up and gave her nipple a sharp tug.

"I don't think I...oh!" Holly's hips moved in a choppy dance of demand. She quivered with his touches, easing his doubts. Angus circled her nub and swished the flat of his tongue over the mass of nerves.

She gave a breathless cry and stiffened, her clit giving a rapid pulse while her sex grasped his fingers. He glanced up at her, and their gazes locked. The intense connection between them sent sheer, desperate need throbbing to his balls. He broke the contact, grabbed a condom, and suited up.

"You said you wanted me to suck you off."

"Changed my mind."

Seconds later, he drove into her with decisive strokes, hard enough to move her up the mattress. Her hands fluttered against his back before settling to grip him close. She'd disobeyed, yet he couldn't use an astringent tone when the jab of her nails into his flesh sparked such heat and longing through him. A tingle boiled in his balls. He thrust once, twice, and the sensation surged up his cock, almost taking his head off with the burst of pleasure. He thought he might have cried out, the spasms of his dick continuing for long moments.

Holly's hands still ran up and down his back, his torso slick now with sweat. Forcing his trembling muscles to hold his weight again, he pulled out of her, making quick work of removing the condom.

The idea of a shower surfaced for about two seconds before he crawled back into bed and reached for Holly. She trusted him with her body, but her mind was lagging in acceptance and that bit. Hurt his pride. He snorted inwardly at that gem. He'd just have to work harder because now that he'd found her, claimed her, he didn't want another man to snatch her away. No, by God, and he wouldn't sit around and let it happen without a fight.

10

PULL UP THE BIG GIRL PANTIES

THE FOLLOWING DAY, HOLLY raced into the call center, breathless and ten minutes late. She settled at her desk, hoping no one had noticed her tardy arrival.

"Hey, Holly." Daniel stopped beside her desk and stood close enough for her to catch his aftershave—something smoky and mysterious. "Did you sleep in this morning?"

"Not exactly," she muttered as she placed on her headphones in preparation to answer the usual barrage.

Her fellow employees were all busy on the phone, politely fielding calls and helping bank customers regarding home loans and other daily banking business. No sooner did they end one than their phone buzzed, signaling another.

"I hit the streets for a run and had a couple of interruptions once I returned home." She focused on her basket of paperwork and scowled at the increased level. It had held two items the previous night.

"Still on for tonight?"

"Of course." She flashed him a smile and prayed he'd decide the heat in her cheeks was fluster because of her lateness. The truth—she felt as if she were cheating on Angus. Heck, in theory, she *was* cheating because she hadn't confessed last night. Oh, no. She'd gone one better and let Angus make love to her, participating fully in giving and receiving pleasure. This morning she'd compounded the error with hot and furious shower sex. It was a wonder she could walk without bowed legs.

"Great, I'll talk to you later."

Holly issued a soft groan, her mind jumping in a dozen different directions, none related to work.

Sabotage.

She was doing an outstanding job of damaging her relationship and felt herself sliding into doubts and insecurity because of her dating history, none of which was Angus's fault. She found her suspicions growing with each phone call for Angus, yet he'd done nothing to warrant her doubts. Heck, the last woman who'd called him—Maggie—was married to Angus's cousin, Connor. She hadn't known until Angus had mentioned having dinner with them since he'd love her to meet his relatives.

Rugby...that was the root of her problem, and it always had been. Despite the great sex with Angus, she kept waiting for the usual issues to develop. The phone calls from other women were already happening. The gossipy stories in the papers and magazines would increase in frequency. Then would come the inevitable explosion where her heart ended up trampled and her emotions swirled in a bloody mess.

She needed to talk to Angus, and soon. She knew it, but that didn't make it easier to approach Angus for a serious discussion. That and their crazy schedules.

THE PLANE LANDED JUST after seven on Monday morning. Holly caught a cab straight to work and strode to her desk to the sound of applause, a real bounce in her step.

"Great game!" Judy called out from the far side of the office.

"Your play was excellent," another girl said.

"Thanks." Holly tugged out her office chair and sat. The game had gone well, her ankle holding up for the ten minutes she'd played on the court toward the end of the match.

"Congratulations," Daniel said from behind her.

She spun her chair to grin up at him. He settled his hands on her shoulders, caging her in the chair, and kissed her on the mouth. The applause, spiced with hearty cheers, restarted, and the instant Daniel retreated, Holly ducked her head, allowing her hair to screen her hot cheeks. "Um, I'd better start work."

Daniel chuckled, squeezed her shoulder, and wandered back to his desk with a swagger to his step.

Judy leaned over and whispered, "I approve. I knew Daniel was interested, but I didn't think he'd move at this speed."

"Ah, thanks," Holly mumbled at a loss. This was terrible. She'd gone to the movies with Daniel last week, and now he'd made assumptions. Not unfounded ones either, given her lack of spine. She needed to talk to Daniel, to Angus.

To her relief, the rest of the day passed rapidly, and after pleading tiredness, she left the others to their after-work socializing at the pub to walk home.

Part of her expected Angus would be there, but the apartment was empty apart from a hint of his citrus aftershave. Relief flooded her along with determination as she set the newspaper and mail on the kitchen counter. She couldn't continue this way. No, it was time for some plain speaking. Tonight when Angus arrived home, she'd tell him about Daniel.

The phone rang, and she answered.

"Holly?"

"Yes." Holly frowned at the familiar voice.

"It's Karen. Is Angus there?"

"No."

"Oh, can you tell him I called?"

"Sure."

"Ah, I need to apologize to you."

"Me?" What on earth did Karen mean?

"Yeah, I saw you the other night at the movies. You were with another guy."

Holly shifted, and her grip on the phone tightened. She didn't want to discuss her man difficulties with this woman.

"I did push you."

It took a few seconds for Karen's blunt words to pierce Holly's irritation. "What?"

"I was jealous. My parents always tell me to keep a grip on my temper. If I had waited...it's obvious you and Angus are simply friends. I'm sorry. Tell Angus I rang, okay?"

The phone clicked, disconnecting the call. A shock of cold rippled across her skin, horror coating her rush of thoughts.

Karen *had* pushed her because of jealousy.

She shuffled to the bedroom and changed into a pair of jeans and a thick woolen jumper. Back in the kitchen, she poured herself a glass of red wine and set about chopping vegetables to make soup.

Thunk. Thunk. Thunk.

Karen...she wasn't sure what to think. She pictured the woman and cut down on a carrot with her knife. By the time the carrot lay in even slices, her anger pulsed like a live wire.

Angus—she wanted to hurl her anger at him, but no. *Not his fault.* He hadn't told Karen to get physical and shove her. Blast it. She picked up the phone and rang her coach, telling her everything she'd discovered.

When she hung up, Holly didn't feel any better. Payback didn't make matters right, didn't return the lost playing time, didn't dial back time so she could play in front of the selectors. *Damn, Karen and her jealousy.*

Restless, she opened the newspaper and flicked past the headlines, scanning stories and occasionally pausing until she reached the sports pages. Anything to occupy her mind. Although she'd heard the results of most of the weekend games, she rechecked them.

"We've gone up on the points table," she said in surprise. "Excellent."

She flicked over the page and pulled a face. The gossip column. She was about to move on to the world news when she spotted a story about Brooke and Sebastian. The photo was an old one, but Brooke looked happy. *Huh.* Just speculation about the sudden marriage of a couple who'd experienced a rocky, on-again, off-again relationship.

The timer buzzed, and Holly stood to check her soup. From the corner of her eye, she caught another familiar face. Detouring, she grabbed the paper and studied the photo of Angus with a dark-haired woman.

A muttered curse slipped past her tight lips as she stomped over to silence the timer. She glared at her pot of soup and switched off the heat while she battled for calm. Her gaze darted to the newspaper. There was no need to read the accompanying story. She'd toss it in the bin and ignore the woman with her hands all over Angus. She'd disregard their easy intimacy.

"Damn it."

They'd slipped into her head now—those grainy black and white figures who looked way too comfortable together, way too involved for her peace of mind. Her feet took her back to study the photo without her permission. Yes, relaxed and happy. Her hands balled to fists at her sides, and burning jealousy flared to life, constricting her chest, pummeling her confidence. In a quick burst of temper, she swiped at the newspaper and watched it land on the floor. He'd promised her...

Oh, hell. Without a murmur of protest, she'd let Daniel kiss her goodnight on Friday. And she'd compounded the foolishness with another kiss in front of witnesses today. Karen knew about her and Daniel.

The bitch.

Holly hadn't believed Coach when she'd said Karen had pushed her on purpose. Holly's conviction of Karen's innocence had led to a temporary suspension. Well, now she'd put an end to the speculation. Karen's confession had sealed her fate.

Her gut bounced around like a netball during drills, the war of anger and guilt and anxiety helping her appetite to flee. Instead of eating, she poured another glass of wine and planted herself on the sofa. She hit the remote, and the television burst into life.

The entire time she kept shooting glances at the newspaper, the annoying, troublemaking part of her wanting to stomp over there, snatch it off the floor, and read the brief article about Angus and the woman in its entirety.

"But that would be silly. I'd just be torturing myself," she muttered.

Things were bad enough now. She didn't even know if he'd come home yet. She hadn't thought to check if his bags were in his bedroom.

A key sounded in the door, and her head jerked in that direction. Her heart beat a little faster as Angus stepped inside, an overnight bag in his left hand.

"I thought your game was on Saturday."

"It was," Angus said. "There was a problem with our flight, and the planes were full. We let the married guys fly out first, but the backlog took hours to clear."

"You look tired."

"The hotel they put us in had thin walls." He rubbed his hand over his jaw, the rasp of stubble loud in the silence.

His bloodshot eyes and drawn face told of his exhaustion. Now wasn't the right time to hit him with accusations and confessions. Holly swallowed and repeated the move since the lump lodged halfway up her windpipe refused to budge.

"We need to talk." She gulped. So much for keeping her mouth shut.

His sharp scrutiny skewered her—the sort of look that made her want to stare at her feet instead of maintaining steady eye contact. An honest gaze. Her stomach quivered with a rush of nerves—that uncontrolled netball again.

"Can I grab a beer first?"

"Ah, sure."

"Do you want more wine?"

"Thanks." Something to do with her hands. Alcohol to gulp for extra courage.

"What's the newspaper doing on the floor?" He squatted to pick up the loose pages and stilled. This time his regard held silent questions.

Unable to bite her tongue for a second longer, she jumped to her feet and started pacing. "Who's the woman?" *Damn, this wasn't the way.* "I had a date on Friday night. I...I thought I should tell you."

"We decided to discuss dating someone else—before the fact." The end of his sentence reverberated throughout the apartment, his words sharp and clipped. Angus slapped the newspaper he'd gathered onto the tabletop and stalked toward her.

Holly backed up until the wall at her spine brought her

to an abrupt halt.

"Did you sleep with him?"

"No!"

"Did you let him kiss you?"

"I...yes. This isn't about me. What about the photo in the paper?"

"It's an old one. That's Marlene Chambers."

"Miss New Zealand?"

"Yes," he said with a touch of impatience. "I haven't seen Marlene in months, not since she left to model overseas. I have no fuckin' idea why they published our picture. You kissed this guy because you're jealous of an old picture?"

Holly sucked in a harsh breath as guilt slapped her around. "No, I told you I went out with Daniel on Friday. I'm sorry."

His glare told her *sorry* didn't cut it. "I'm going to take a shower."

"Karen rang for you."

"Why?"

"How should I know? She confessed, though."

"What are you talking about?"

"Karen pushed me on purpose during the game because she thought you and I were an item. She was jealous."

"You're joking." Incredulous, he stared at her, maybe waiting for a punch line.

"She was serious. She injured me because of you."

"*Fuck.* Damn, I'm sorry. I had no idea. Believe me."

"It's screwed up my chances of making the Silver Ferns this year."

Angus spat out another curse and abruptly left the room, leaving Holly pacing alone. She tipped the contents of her glass down her throat. He wasn't responsible for Karen's actions, even though her netball career would suffer the setback. Now she'd told him about Daniel, so why the heck didn't she feel better?

HOLLY STARED INTO THE darkness several hours later, then turned onto her right side and huddled into the blankets. The shivers wouldn't stop. So much for flannel pajamas. It was bloody freezing in her bedroom.

For ten minutes longer, she tossed and turned, her mind too busy for sleep. Finally, in frustration, she switched on the light and checked her clock. Quarter to six. She'd go for a run. Hopefully, she'd decide what to do by the time she arrived back at the apartment.

Outside, light from the streetlamps pierced the early morning fog coming off the water. Holly did a sequence of stretches before she jogged along the pavement toward the park. This upheaval was her fault. Remorse ate at her, echoed with every strike of her shoes against the damp sidewalk.

Angus hadn't returned after his shower. Instead, he'd

gone into his bedroom and shut the door. She'd screwed up her courage and sneaked a peek inside after an hour of silence and found him asleep.

While she'd stewed in alternative self-regrets and irritation—a guilty conscience—he'd been busily punching out Zs.

In deference to her ankle, she kept to her recent routine of a shorter run and returned to the apartment. With her heart in her mouth, she opened the door to a coffee hit.

Angus stood in the kitchen, dressed in jeans and an old rugby shirt, a mug cupped in his hands.

"Good morning," she said, the chocolatey notes of coffee making her crave caffeine.

"You cheated on me."

"It was a date," she snapped, shame giving her words a defensive bite.

"You let him kiss you."

Holly closed her eyes, no longer feeling like breakfast or a beverage. A coffee would hit her gut and spurt right back up, given the churning of her stomach. "I'm sorry," she repeated, unable to meet his gaze. Her breathing turned choppy and audible, and her pulse raced.

"Did you sleep with him too?"

"No, I've already told you I didn't. I'm not lying! We kissed after he walked me to the door. That's it." It didn't seem right to tell him about the kiss in the office, too.

"Did you want to take things further with him?" His

raw tone demanded answers, honesty.

"No." She glanced up and caught the twist of his lips. "I'm telling you the truth."

"That's something, at least. I thought you were happy with our relationship."

"I was. I am."

"Then why did you go out with him? We agreed we'd tell each other if we wanted out of this arrangement. Make me understand."

Holly's mouth felt as if someone had stuffed it with a dry sock. She swallowed and skirted his still form to pour a glass of water. God, she'd made such a mess of things. She should have told him about her past—the whole truth about her lousy record with rugby players.

"I...I don't want to be late to work."

"You have plenty of time."

Sighing, Holly took a seat at the breakfast counter. A mistake. She needed the motion to get through this in one piece. She took a slug of water, held it in her mouth for a second, and swallowed. After setting down the glass, she shot to her feet and paced. "I've had three boyfriends since moving to Auckland."

"You've told me that before, and I told you not to foist their crap on me."

Damn, he was right. She knew it but try telling her heart to use commonsense.

She inhaled and started talking. "I moved in with Brooke

at age seventeen. I needed to be in the city to play for a top team and gain the notice of the Dynamo selectors. I left school and got a job at the bank to pay my way. Mark, my first boyfriend, broke my heart. He wanted to marry me and have kids, which was fine, but he wanted kids sooner rather than later."

"And that didn't work because you wanted to play netball."

"Yes. I might have been okay if I'd made the team first, then fallen pregnant and taken a few months off, but I needed to make my way up the ranks. I told Mark I didn't want children—at least not so soon—and he broke off our relationship. There was no middle ground for him."

"I've supported you—your netball—from the moment you moved in with me." Angus bored holes through her with his glare.

"Yes, you have." The acknowledgment layered more guilt onto her tense shoulders. "My second boyfriend was Brad Donald."

"I can guess what happened with him. He's incapable of commitment to one woman."

A pang of self-pity crashed through her. Oh, yes. It'd taken her ages to realize what he hid beneath his charm. "You know about Craig. He was the third, and he didn't bother telling me about the girlfriend he had stashed in his hometown."

"I have not slept with another woman since I met you."

Ice dripped from the words. "Hell, I haven't looked at another woman."

Holly stopped pacing, fixed him with a stare. "But this thing between us is temporary. That's what you told me when we discussed it. You might not have used those exact words, but you implied them." He wasn't even calling her by those stupid endearments anymore, and she missed them. How silly was that?

"Fuck, fuck, *fuck*." Angus dragged a hand through his hair before lifting his head to glare at her yet again.

She swallowed, her shoulders stiff while guilt continued to churn through her mind and kill her appetite.

The phone rang, breaking their impasse.

Angus reached over to answer. "Yes," he barked into the receiver. He extended it to Holly. "It's for you."

"Hello."

"Holly, have dinner with us tonight," Brooke said. "I want to show you our honeymoon photos. Can you come, or do you have practice?"

"What time?"

"Come after you finish work," Brooke said. "Do you want to invite Angus too?"

"No."

"Oh? Trouble in paradise?"

"No, I'll see you later. Bye." She hung up and handed the phone back to Angus. "I won't be home for dinner."

Fury flashed in his eyes as he slammed the phone back

into its cradle. "Are you going out on another date with him?"

"No."

His stare sliced and diced. "This thing between us is not temporary. I want you, and I thought you wanted me too."

11

A DOSE OF TRUTH

LATER THAT MORNING, HOLLY picked up her pen and twirled it, her mind on Angus's last words. If he wanted her, then why hadn't he told her earlier?

Because you would've freaked out.

Angus had read her well, treating her like a wary animal until she became comfortable with him. Instead of appreciating the small ways he helped her every day—the way Angus cooked meals or picked her up from training or gave her small gifts or simply talked through training issues, she'd panicked, painting him with the sins of previous boyfriends.

She squeezed her eyes shut for a pained instant. Hell, was it any wonder she doubted her ability to pick the right man with her previous record? She wished she could've talked to Angus, but he'd been asleep, and she hadn't liked to wake him since he'd looked exhausted.

Daniel stopped by her desk, his smile fading when he noted her expression. "Are you okay?"

"Nothing a few hours of sleep won't fix," she said with a rueful smile.

"So you don't want to go out tonight?"

Holly glanced away from his hopeful face to focus on the stack of papers on her desk. This couldn't continue. At this rate, she'd hurt Daniel too. "No, how about a quick coffee together later?"

Daniel brightened, and she hated herself. She was as bad as her ex-boyfriends, given the way she was blundering through emotional minefields. "What about lunch?"

"I'm rostered for a break at twelve," she said.

"Great, me too. I'll meet you then."

But he mightn't talk to her later, not after she finished telling him about Angus and how she'd misled them both.

The morning flew with phone calls, taking up much of her time. At twelve on the dot, Daniel headed in her direction. Ignoring the unpleasant lurch of nerves, she finished with her current customer and switched her calls to the central system. "Let's go," she said, plucking her handbag from under her desk.

Daniel ushered her to the street level. "Where would you like to eat?"

"Anywhere that serves coffee. I need something to keep me awake."

"This way." He led her toward the café on the corner with the garden out the back.

A group of businessmen laughed with hearty guffaws. A white parrot in a cage squawked at a child who stuck his grubby fingers through the wire. The mother should watch her kid because that parrot had a disturbing gleam in its eye.

Holly risked another glance at Daniel. The way he kept smiling stoked her nerves to fever-pitch. A light film of sweat, fueled by fear, coated her skin. Her atrocious behavior would hurt him, and she hoped he'd speak to her after she showered him with the truth. She was with Angus.

Idiot. God, she was so stupid. She'd upset two fantastic and decent men with one strike.

"What sort of coffee?"

"Latte, please," she said, not even battling to pay her way. She took possession of an empty table and sank into a chair. Knives and forks clattered against china plates in a discordant rhythm. The scent of sweet peas floated to her from the nearby trellis, the fragrance of the red and purple flowers reminding her of Angus's ridiculous endearments. Shame twisted her belly, and she ripped her gaze away to stare at her plain black shoes.

Minutes later, Daniel joined her, an order number in his hand. "You still don't look very well."

She hesitated and inhaled to the count of four before

slowly releasing it to calm herself. "Rough night. Daniel, I'm sorry, but I can't go out with you again." She took in his disappointed expression and sped up to get everything out. "I can't give you more than friendship."

No, no, *no*. The edge of determination creeping onto his features spelled conflict, and alarm flared in her.

"Why?"

"There's someone else."

"You didn't think to tell me that before? Who?"

Knots filled her throat, and she had to swallow hard to get the words out. "My roomie."

"O'Neil?"

She gave a clipped nod, her sigh loud in the pulsing and anger-filled silence. "I've made a real mess of this, and you have every right to be furious with me. This wasn't my finest moment, and I'm so sorry for my poor behavior."

A young man with a whip-thin body and purple hair delivered their coffee, his arrival a welcome interruption to the rising tension.

"Thanks," Holly said and waited until the man departed. "Look, I've behaved badly. I'm really, really sorry and hope you'll forgive my lapse in judgment. I'll go." She fumbled in her bag for her wallet.

Daniel's hand clamped on her forearm. "Stay."

She froze and forced her muscles to relax back into her chair. "I'm so sorry."

"After our kiss the other night, I guessed something was

wrong." He shot her a wry grin. "You didn't seem eager, not in the same way as me."

Well, at least she'd done something right. "I'm sorry."

"Stop apologizing. If you ever kick O'Neil to the curb, I'll be here."

She frowned, feeling snake-belly low, and wished with all her might she could have a do-over. Unfortunately, life didn't work that way. She'd acted stupidly and hurt two honorable men in the process. "Now you're making me feel guilty. I wish you'd shout at me."

"Think of it as a punishment," he said with a quick grin to negate the sentiment. "I'm going to grab a sandwich. Do you want one?"

"No. Thanks."

Daniel had taken her news with graciousness and civility, not that it improved her mindset. If anything, her remorse intensified. She'd never been this woman who toyed with men and used them like players on a sports field, and she hated the position she found herself in now. Her stupid behavior filled her with self-loathing.

INSTEAD OF GOING TO Seb and Brooke's apartment straight after work, Holly detoured to Angus's place, wanting to speak with him and apologize. She clattered up the stairs in preference to the elevator, gnarled knots filling her throat while she planned what to say. Her palms dripped with nerves, and she wiped them several times on her black trousers. But Holly didn't let her anxiety derail her mission. She planned to speak with Angus and make things right or attempt to explain her stupid behavior, her insecurity, and dumb decision-making.

The minute she opened the apartment door, the silent emptiness told her he wasn't present. It wasn't a practice night, so where was he? She prowled the apartment for twenty minutes before a glimpse of the clock had her scurrying to her room to do a quick change into jeans, her favorite pink shirt, and a denim jacket.

She snatched up her bag and ran out the door, catching the bus after a breathless race to the stop halfway along the street. Of course, the bus was standing room only. Holly crammed between a thin man with dreadful BO and a woman who'd stopped at the supermarket. The bunch of bananas at the top of her shopping bag was way past the stage of ripeness Holly preferred, and she wrinkled her nose, reduced to careful breaths through her mouth to survive the bus ride.

"You're late," Brooke said when she opened the door.

"Sorry. At the last moment, I hustled back to the apartment and changed. The bus took ages." More lies to avoid the truth. "I can't wait to hear about your honeymoon—the family-friendly parts," she said at Brooke's sly grin.

Her sister grasped her arm and led her into a beautiful designer kitchen. Exotic spices filled the air, and Holly's stomach gurgled a demand for food. Seb stood at the stove, stirring a pot. Soft orchestral music came from a Bluetooth speaker.

Holly blinked. Seb and cooking—together. Color her shocked. "Hi, Seb. You're looking good."

"You mean healthy, right?" Brooke teased her. "You're not eyeing up my husband."

"I only have eyes for you, darling," he said, winking at his wife.

"Brooke! I mean that you both seem puke-inducing happy. I'm pleased for you, even if you cheated me out of bridesmaid duties."

"We didn't want a fuss or the publicity, but I would've chosen a kick-arse dress for you." Brooke beamed at her. "You know that, right?"

"She says that now," Holly said to Seb, adding a wink. "What's for dinner? It smells great."

"A lamb casserole with couscous. I'm making soup for a starter."

The evening passed pleasantly as she caught up with their news, admired the photos, and ate a delicious meal.

"Stay the night," Brooke said.

"No, I have training straight after work tomorrow. It'll be easier if I go home now." She intended to speak with Angus, no matter how late. If she had to wait for him to come home, she would, but she had to make him see she regretted her behavior.

Damn, she'd grovel if necessary. This uncomfortable avoidance between them now was all on her. She was the one who'd let her past stomp over the present.

Angus hadn't deserved her dishonesty.

She mentally toted up her cash and decided to call a ride. She'd make her lunch and cut out coffee and drinks for the rest of the week.

"I'll call a cab," she said.

Brooke stared at her in shock. "A cab?"

"Yes. Besides, you guys don't need me around. I'll wait until you reach your month anniversary until I crash here."

Despite Brooke's arguments, Holly headed home. Braced for darkness and silence, plus the possibility of a long wait, the murmur of voices from the lounge came as a pleasant surprise. Angus was at home and still awake.

Well, here goes.

She sucked in a fortifying breath and burst into the room, a wide smile on her lips as she mentally prepared an apology and her explanation for her behavior.

"Angus, I—" She broke off abruptly on recognizing Angus's guest. Shock ripped her smile away, and a spear of pain shot her straight in the heart. "Sorry, I didn't mean to interrupt."

"You're not intruding," Angus said in a smooth voice.

His expression lacked his usual charm and warmth, and

something in Holly twisted before dying a nasty death. She'd done this—made way for another woman with her stupid doubts.

"Have you met Marlene Chambers? Marlene, this is Holly Blackwood, my roomie."

Marlene's well-defined brows arched in surprise. "I didn't realize you were sharing your accommodation."

Marlene was classically beautiful with a smooth sweep of glossy brown hair, bright blue eyes, and dimples. Topped off with a slim figure, which she'd showcased tonight in tight blue jeans and a breast-hugging Angora jumper in mint green, it was easy to understand why she'd won the Miss New Zealand title.

"Holly plays for the Blue Dynamos. We're both away a lot, and sharing works for us," Angus said.

"Nice to meet you, Marlene." Holly forced out the polite words and attempted to contain her jealousy. The required nonchalance proved difficult. "I have an early start tomorrow morning, so I'd better get some sleep." She turned away, intent on making her escape.

"How was Daniel?" Angus asked.

Holly forced herself to face Angus. She met his gaze and zapped him with the truth. "I had dinner at Seb and Brooke's place, remember? Daniel and I are friends, and that's all we'll ever be. No chemistry on my end."

A ripple of light laughter emerged from Marlene, full of musical amusement. "Ouch."

"He's okay with that?" Angus demanded.

"Yes." She'd made a colossal mistake, and now she was paying for her stupid behavior. "Good night. Nice to meet you, Marlene."

By the time she reached her bedroom, unshed tears stung her eyes, and her bottom lip throbbed where she'd bitten down to keep her composure. On automatic, she started her bedtime routine, the ache in her chest making breathing difficult. Her lack of trust had done this. The words beat at her until her head ached at the *bang, bang, bang* of her regrets. The consequences were all on her.

Once in bed, she stared into the darkness and tried not to imagine what was happening in the lounge. They'd appeared awful cozy with the partially empty bottle of wine sitting on the counter. At least she hadn't interrupted a romantic clinch, but she didn't have a problem imagining the pair kissing or doing more.

Together, they made a stunning couple. A sob escaped. Holly turned over on her side, curled into a ball of misery, and cried into her pillow.

She must have fallen asleep because an out-of-the-ordinary creak jerked her to consciousness. For long seconds, she froze while she attempted to ferret out the identity of the noise. Frowning, she fumbled for the lamp and flicked it on.

"Angus? What are you doing? Where's Marlene?"

Angus unbuckled his belt and pulled it out of his jeans.

"I sent her home." He unbuttoned his shirt.

Holly clutched the covers to her chest, watching him in confusion. "What are you doing?"

"I'm getting undressed."

"I can see that," Holly said with a trace of sarcasm. "Why?"

Angus peeled off his boxer-briefs and, naked pulled back the covers on the bed and slid in beside her. She was too stunned to do anything more than gape at him.

"What about Marlene?"

He rearranged the pillows and settled against them. "Marlene wanted to slot back into the relationship we'd had before she decided to pursue a modeling career overseas. I told her I wasn't interested. I told her there was someone else."

"Me?" Holly squeaked.

He was in bed with her. Naked. Did that mean he'd decided to give her a second chance? She considered him for a fraction longer. "Are you giving me another chance?"

A pained expression etched into his features as he met her gaze. "I'm so damn sorry about Karen. I had no idea she was capable of something like this."

"It's not your fault. You didn't push me."

"I know, but I wish I could fix this for you. What will you do about Karen?"

"I've informed the coach, and she can do as she sees fit. The truth—if I see Karen, she'd better watch for my right hook."

Angus barked out his amusement before his smile faded. "I want to marry you, Holly."

"What?" Shock zapped her, leaving her trembling. Uncertain. "But I've screwed up."

"You did," he said, sweeping a lock of hair off her face with gentle fingers. "But I have too—you're not entirely at fault. Maybe I should've made my intentions clearer instead of giving you time to become used to the idea of us as a couple." He sighed. "You're not the only one with a failed relationship. You know I'm divorced?"

"Yes, it's no secret, but you never talk about your ex-wife."

Angus pulled a face. "No. Young men and women, too, sometimes equate lust with love. Louise and I met when things were starting to go okay for me. Selectors had picked me for the senior team. I was playing well and improving different facets of my game. Louise and I didn't sleep together before we married, and after the wedding, the lovemaking didn't go well."

Holly gaped at him. "But you're an awesome lover. Everything we do together is fun and so damn hot. You're giving, and always make sure I enjoy our time together."

"Thank you." He clasped her fingers and smoothed this thumb over the back of her hand. "Back to my marriage. Whenever I wanted to try something different in bed, Louise would call me a deviant. Let's just say the divorce a year later was a relief for both of us. After that, I dated women and had sex, but I was careful. Until you, no one tempted me to try for more. It was simple to see you were wary. I suggested friends and, at first, suspected our dating would run its course. I thought we'd both move on, which was what I'd been doing since my divorce. All my relationships were short-lived."

Her heart raced, and her belly fluttered as she met his gaze. "Your friends-with-benefits plan was a ruse?"

"I wanted to spend time with you." He huffed out a heavy sigh and what might've been regret. "You're gorgeous, and you fascinated me when we first met. Once you moved in with me, I discovered you're uncomplicated to live with, you keep up with me sexually, and you understand my drive to play rugby. Sweetheart, you're perfect for me."

He'd called her sweetheart, and the endearment was spot-on. A tear ran over her cheek, a tight sensation clamping around her chest and making her fight for breath. "I'm so sorry about the way I handled things with Daniel. I hate that I hurt you."

"We've both made mistakes. I can't say I'm relaxed about you working with the guy, but as long as you keep coming home to me and share my bed, I'll live with the idea."

"You'd trust me after the way I've behaved?" Holly gave an unladylike sniff, unable to believe his generosity.

"Yes, but I guess we'll need to work on our

communication. I want a future with you, Holly. I want to celebrate the good and commiserate on the bad things that might happen to you. Can we start over, agree to be exclusive, and see where things go?"

"Oh, Angus." She threw herself at him, wrapped her arms around his broad shoulders, and clung. "Yes. Yes, please."

He made a pained sound deep in his throat and kissed her with feral hunger. Her arms curled around his neck, and she held on for dear life, kissing him back with equal fervor.

He pulled back, climbed out of bed, and lifted her off the mattress in one smooth motion. "We'll sleep in my bed," he said. "*Our* bed, and we'll celebrate with passionate sex."

"Sounds perfect to me."

"Did I mention I hate these blue pajamas?"

"I'll burn them," she promised.

In his bedroom, he followed her onto the mattress and made quick work of separating her from her flannel pajamas. He started kissing her, his hot mouth seducing her while his talented hands created havoc. A pleasurable ache settled low between her thighs, growing with each stroke of his fingers, each pluck of her breast, and nibble at her throat. Swept off her feet, Holly struggled to keep up, yearning to touch him in return and reassure herself she wasn't dreaming.

His mouth created a heated path, and when his lips

finally surrounded her nipple, tongued it, and sucked, she let out a desperate moan.

"Angus, please."

"I intend to please you, sweetheart. You'll never forget we're meant for each other."

"You're going to kill me," she said. "It's possible to die of pleasure. Some of the romance novels say so."

"I'm going to love you," he corrected and fumbled for the bedside drawer. He lifted his head, pulled out a strip of condoms, and ripped one off. Seconds later, he pushed inside her. He set a fast and furious pace, kissing, touching, and loving her relentlessly.

Holly soared. She clutched his shoulders and gave him everything, her body, her heart, her soul. And as the beginnings of her climax swept her into passion, she realized the emotions roiling through her were happiness and the giddy sense of success.

Their relationship might have started as a friendly game with two opponents, but the result was a win for both competitors.

12

THE UNDERWEAR SHOOT AND NOSY GOSSIP

ANGUS AND HOLLY RAN together the following morning. The winter rain had subsided and made way for a crisp but fine morning with the promise of sun and warmth if one found a seat out of the wind. The strike of their feet on the sidewalk pavement and the purr of car engines from early commuters was the only sound. Holly floated along, buoyed by her happiness, and even though she and Angus didn't talk, she enjoyed his undemanding company.

When they reached the park, Angus broke the silence between them. "Are you doing your normal sprints?"

"Just a few," she said. "I'm still babying my ankle."

He nodded. "I'll do a couple of circuits before I head

back. Will you return with me or run for longer?"

Holly smiled at him. "I'm going to do my stretch routine first. See you at home?"

He stopped running, and she turned, jogging on the spot to see what he was doing.

"I'll be busy for most of the day and won't get home tonight until late." He pulled a face. "Sponsorship stuff. We're filming an underwear ad and making nice with the sponsors and other participants afterward at a dinner."

A laugh burst from Holly. "No! That sounds awful."

Angus grimaced. "Just so you know, there will be female models there as well, but I'm not interested in any of them. It's you who does it for me."

"I'm pleased to hear that. Angus." She paused. "Thanks for telling me. Trust is hard for me. I'm afraid I'm a work in progress."

Angus growled. "You're working with him."

Holly met his gaze. "I know, but Daniel and I will never be anything but friends. If you can, why don't you come along for drinks with my work crowd? I'd like that."

"It's a date as soon as we can manage it."

Holly reached up to kiss his cheek. "I'll look forward to hearing about your photo session and the gossip."

Angus pulled a face. "Today will *not* be my idea of fun." He hugged her and claimed a kiss, plundering her mouth for long, breath-stealing moments. "Are we letting people know we're a couple?"

"Yes." Holly never hesitated, and warmth filled her chest, her mind, her heart. Angus's bright and approving smile boosted her feel-good mood.

"Excellent. Can you come to my game on Friday night? It's our last home game before the end of the season."

"We have a bye this week. I'd love to watch you play," Holly said.

"Right. I'll organize a ticket for you. And on that note, I'd better hustle. I'm not sure what time I'll be home."

They parted ways, and Holly ran sprints. She was pleased with her ankle and considered doing more than the two sets of three she'd allowed herself.

"No," she said and started her stretches. "Don't tempt fate." Once she'd finished, she jogged back to the apartment and grabbed a copy of the paper before she went upstairs. A glance at the kitchen clock told her she had plenty of time to shower, change for work, and have a leisurely breakfast.

She hummed her way through a shower and dressed in chocolate brown pants and a copper-colored blouse Maria had bought for her during her parents' last visit to the city. She teamed this with the matching brown jacket and a pair of low-heeled ankle boots.

In the kitchen, she switched on the radio. Angus had set up the coffee machine for her with a cup, and to the side sat a single apricot-colored rose. Her lips parted in a soft, "Oh."

The coffee and rose were small things, but his thoughtfulness made her heart go pitter-patter. Angus's care when he was busy and rushing to do his sponsorship gig brought home to her how lucky she was to have him in her life.

Aware of the passing time, Holly ate cereal and drank her coffee while checking her email. The manager of their netball team had sent a message asking them to attend a team meeting tomorrow evening. There went her plans to make a special dinner for Angus. Perhaps she'd make something he could cook once he arrived home, even if she couldn't eat the meal with him.

Pleased with her idea, she cleared away her breakfast dishes, grabbed her handbag and keys, and left for work.

This morning, she was five minutes early, but she started work straight away to make up for her recent tardiness. She waved to the others as they arrived and continued working. It didn't take long for her to feel strange looks boring into her, and for brief seconds, she wondered if she'd buttoned her blouse wrong or had some other clothing malfunction. A quick check confirmed her appearance was satisfactory.

The weird looks continued, and finally Holly shrugged them off. She kept working until Daniel approached her just before morning tea.

"Are you taking a break now?" he asked.

"Yes, a cup of tea sounds like heaven," she said. "My voice is croaky from talking so long to the last customer."

She hesitated. "Is it my imagination, or is everyone looking at me strangely?"

Daniel paused for a long moment. "They're curious."

"About what? Not about us?"

"No, I told them we're friends and nothing more. It's... There's a story in the newspaper."

Holly rolled her eyes. "About Angus? Most of those stories comprise old photos and innuendo."

"It's about you and Angus," Daniel said carefully.

"But..." She shrugged. "I decided yesterday I'm not reading anything Angus-related, and I refuse to read about myself. I'd never agree to an interview, not unless it related to netball or sponsorship."

She hoped the article contained nothing to upset Angus. Immediately, a sense of shame filled her. She'd judged Angus on the things written in some of those articles. She'd heard Brooke mutter when she and Seb had made the headlines, usually during one of their breakups. These thoughts and her conversation with Angus the previous night made her determined to hold hard to her decision. She refused to get drawn into the world of gossip and innuendo again. That way lay madness and heartbreak.

"So you don't have a child?" Daniel asked.

Holly gaped at him. "No! Angus and I only started dating this year."

"With Craig Hammond," Daniel said.

She shuddered. "Heck, no! I might have dated the

creep, but that was all." Ugh! Holly was beginning to understand Angus's frustration with the newspapers and magazines. "I'm glad I didn't read the paper this morning." And she wouldn't read it, she reiterated to herself yet again. The important people in her life—Angus and her family—knew her opinion of Craig Hammond. They also understood that if she ever had a child, she wouldn't hide the kid away or adopt or anything else. One day, she hoped to have children with Angus as their father, but it would be when they were ready.

She stood, transferring her calls back to central before she smiled at Daniel. "Are you taking fifteen now?"

"Sure," he said. "I don't suppose I could entice you into going with me to the new action film out next week?"

"I'd love to go, but I'd need to check with Angus. I don't want him to think I'm sneaking around behind his back," she said. "Maybe we can see if any of the others are interested?"

Daniel nodded at her. "Fair enough. I'm looking forward to meeting Angus."

"I asked him if he wanted to come out with us for drinks later in the week. He said it depends on rugby commitments." She beamed at Daniel as they walked into the lunchroom.

"You're taking this well," Judy said, her face full of concern. "It can't be very nice having your private life splashed over the page for everyone to read."

Holly scowled. "I refuse to read unfounded gossip. It's the usual clickbait. I have never had a child."

"I thought you said Angus was your roomie," Judy said.

"He is, but we're also dating."

"You stole him from Miss New Zealand?" Judy's voice rose toward the end of her sentence. "Wow! That was a ballsy move!"

Holly barked out a laugh, but it held little amusement. "What? No! Angus and I met at a party. There was no stealing or anything else going on. We liked each other and eventually started dating. That's all I'm saying on the subject since my private life works better for me if it remains private. Daniel and I were discussing the new action film coming out this week. We're both addicted to action films and want to see this latest one. I'm going to ask Angus if he wants to go. Are you in?"

"Ooh! Is that the one with that tall blond Aussie guy?" Judy asked.

Daniel chuckled. "That's the one."

"I'm in," Judy said. "It's always more fun to go in a group."

"Great," Holly said.

"Holly, do you have a moment?" Susan Webb, her immediate boss, stood in the lunchroom's doorway.

"Sure." Holly stood and followed Susan to her office.

When Susan gestured her inside and shut the door behind them, nerves jumped around Holly's stomach.

"Have I done something wrong?"

"No, of course not," Susan said and gestured her to a seat. "Coffee?"

Something in Holly relaxed at the kindness in Susan's expression. "That would be lovely." She waited while Susan placed a capsule into the machine and inhaled the heavenly fragrance with appreciation. Meanwhile, her curiosity went on a rampage.

Once they had cups of coffee in front of them, Susan smiled at her. "I'm presuming the story in the paper this morning has little basis in fact."

Holly grimaced. "I haven't read the story and don't intend to anytime soon." She glanced at her boss and wondered how much she should say.

"Do you know Angus's cousin, Connor?"

Bemused at the shift in the conversation, Holly shook her head. "Angus has mentioned him, but I haven't met him yet."

"Connor and his wife, Maggie, are good friends of mine. Do you remember the reality show *Farmer Seeks a Wife*?" Susan asked.

Holly's eyes went wide. It had been a few years ago now when she was still at school, but she suddenly understood why her boss seemed so familiar. She clapped her hand across her mouth.

Susan grinned. "Yep. Mr. Blue, the vibrator. I got such a hard time since most of the New Zealand viewing public watched the show. Facts got twisted," Susan said. "My point is that I've met Angus twice now, and I know he is a lot like his cousin and is a great guy. From what I've seen of you, you're hardworking and dedicated to your sport. Are you dating Angus?"

"Yes," Holly said. "It's been difficult seeing stories and hearing rumors, and they've caused trouble between Angus and me. You're right when you say Angus is an amazing man. He's smart and genuine. We've talked, and I trust him, which is why I stopped reading the gossip pages."

"A wise move," Susan said with approval. "Can I ask a nosy question?"

Holly nodded. "Yes, but I reserve the right not to answer."

"Fair enough. How serious are you and Angus?"

"It's early days yet, but we're committed to each other, and we'll see where that takes us. Will this publicity be a problem for my job?"

"No," Susan said. "But if you ever need anyone to talk to or just sound off, call me. I'll introduce you to my other friends. We all have our stories and understand what you're going through."

"Thank you. From the little I've gleaned, it sounds as if the reporter has taken a few facts and twisted them out of shape."

"Exactly," Susan said. "All you need is to add an alien to

the mix, and there's enough to make a decent soap opera."

Holly frowned. "That bad?"

"Yes. I have your number. I'll call you when my friends and I are having our next get-together. Hopefully, Angus will be around and can come too."

"Thanks."

"It's a date." Susan finished her coffee and stood, indicating their meeting had ended.

Holly worked through to one when she decided to take a walk to clear her head and get away from her coworkers' speculative gazes. She scooped up her phone and handbag and left the building. Her phone rang as she left, and a glance at the screen had her answering straightaway. She stepped out of the way of the foot traffic to a place where she could speak freely.

"Angus, how is your underwear modeling going?"

"We're on a lunch break. Marlene's here, and I've had to pose with her."

Angus sounded angry, and apprehension slid through Holly. "Is something wrong? Is it the newspaper story? I've heard about it, but I haven't read the article. After last night, I decided to avoid the gossip section. It upsets me, and I know most of the stories are a shade of the truth and cause pain for those concerned."

"Sweetheart." Wholehearted approval sounded in his voice. "Marlene let it slip that she'd fed the story to a reporter after she'd met with your ex, Craig, at a party. I wanted to make sure you were okay."

"I am fine, and it's because we made peace last night and my decision to boycott the gossip pages. I also realized the people who matter—you and my family—know the truth, and they'd never believe half of what gets published."

"I miss you," Angus said. "I wish I could steal away now."

"Tonight," Holly said, promise shimmering in her voice. "My boss had a chat with me. Susan said she's met you and is a friend of your cousin's."

"Ah, Susan and Tyler. I didn't connect the dots until now."

"She said she'd invite me to their next gathering," Holly said. "I like her a lot. She's a brilliant boss, and she's fair."

"Even if I'm not here or able to go, you should," Angus said. "You'll like the group of friends. Thank you for not assuming the worst about the article."

"From what I've heard, there's a lot about my love-child. Susan told me if they'd added an alien, it would have soap opera potential."

Angus spluttered and laughed loudly. She held the phone away from her ear and grinned until voices in the background told her they needed Angus.

"I can't wait to kiss you again," he said, his voice low and intimate. "I'll try not to be too late."

"See you tonight," she whispered and waited until she heard the call disconnect.

During her walk, she had phone calls from her parents and Brooke, each indignant about the story's contents.

"I didn't read it, and I'm not going to," she told her parents.

"We're proud of you," her father said.

"I had a feeling there was something between you and Angus," her mother added. "That part of the story is true?"

"Yes, Angus and I are dating. It works because we both have sporting commitments and understand the dedication required to make the top levels. I like Angus a lot."

"I want to meet him," her father said.

Holly didn't hesitate. "If you'd like to come to Angus's match on Friday night, you could meet him then. I can ask Angus if he could get tickets."

"I'll get the tickets. I'll buy one for you so we can sit together. We can watch Brooke doing her cheer routine."

"I'd like that, Dad." Holly hung up with a smile. She hadn't hesitated to introduce Angus to her parents, and that told her a lot, too. Pride bloomed because she was learning to deal with the side effects of rugby and netball fame.

It was a hurried chat with her sister because she'd needed to return to work, but Brooke had shared that she no longer read the gossip pages. Hearsay had caused problems between her and Seb.

Holly strode down the street, her steps slowing on spotting men and women loitering outside her building. They held either microphones and cameras.

"Holly Blackwood!" a woman shouted.

Within seconds, they'd mobbed her.

"Holly," a more familiar voice shouted.

Daniel pushed his way through the mass of reporters firing questions at Holly.

"Is it true you had a child with Craig Hammond?"

"Why do you keep the child hidden?" a female reporter demanded.

"Don't you think it was mean to steal Miss New Zealand's boyfriend?"

"Are you and Angus O'Neil shacked up together?"

Anger flooded Holly at this last question since she and Angus were not *shacked up* together. They were a couple. About to defend herself, she strove for control and pressed her lips together. She didn't owe these reporters a thing.

"Who are you?" another reporter shouted at Daniel.

"Are you Holly's lover?"

"Morons," Daniel muttered in her ear. "Don't feed the monsters. Let's get back to work."

Holly and Daniel pushed through the reporters and past the cameramen and women, saying nothing. The cameras continued rolling as they surged past and into the building foyer.

"Wow, I didn't expect that," Holly said once they were

safely in the elevator.

"I didn't either. I was on my way back from buying an SD card for my camera. You looked as if you needed rescuing."

"I appreciate your help, but you might regret your generosity if they publish our picture."

Daniel snorted. "They'll soon discover I'm not newsworthy."

After work, Holly left via the rear entrance, which emerged into the underground car park. Judy had offered her a lift home, and she was glad when she spotted the number of reporters out the front of the building. When Judy dropped her off, there were only two reporters and one cameraman. She stalked past them and entered her building, using her keycard. She barred a man from following her inside and waited for the door to close, shutting him outdoors.

Hopefully, the journalists would grow tired of this, or a politician would claim their attention with a policy announcement. She required a strategy. Holly entered the apartment while pondering her best course of action. In the end, she decided to cook and relax after a session at the apartment gym.

Angus arrived home at nine-thirty. His expression was grim as he walked into the apartment, and Holly's heart sank.

"Is something wrong?"

"A crappy day, but I'm all the better for seeing you." Angus's arms came around her, and she closed the last bit of distance between them.

His citrus aftershave washed over her, as did a sense of security.

"I know the feeling," she said. "I had reporters chase me back from the walk I took at lunch, not long after I spoke with you. Luckily, Daniel was coming in from an errand, and he helped me get away from the pack. They're like rabid dogs."

Angus chuckled. "Yep, they were lying in wait for me too."

"I've been giving the matter some thought," Holly said. "My suggestion is to grab a couple of different disguises to use for the coming weeks, vary our schedules, and ride out the public interest with no comments. Surround ourselves with people we trust and live our lives as best we can."

"Holly, sweetheart." His voice was soft, gentle. "I love you. No wait," he said, placing his fingers over her mouth. "Let me speak."

Last week, she would've panicked on hearing his declaration, but something had changed in her. Angus had changed her because she trusted him. From the moment he'd come into her life, he'd treated her with respect and given her honesty while she'd fought him every bit of the way.

"Things have happened fast between us, and I

understand you're not ready to give me the words yet. I don't need them straightaway. When we're together, I enjoy every moment, whether we're making love or lazing in front of the TV. You fit into my life like the perfect puzzle piece. When we first met, I was attracted to you, but I wasn't looking for anything serious. It didn't take long for my mind to change. I want you to know I'm all in and looking forward to our future and all it contains."

Tears blurred her vision. Happy tears, and she beamed at him, her heart full. He understood her need for caution, to take time because she'd been burned so often. "Thank you, Angus."

The special words hovered at the tip of her tongue anyway, but when she said them, she wanted to make them unique and meaningful in a way neither she nor Angus would ever forget. A moment she'd always recall.

"You're very welcome, sweetheart." And he kissed her again before sweeping her off her feet and heading toward their bedroom.

Holly nestled in his arms, at peace and yet excited for the future with Angus. She thought she'd say those words to him soon.

Very soon.

13

A GLIMPSE OF THE FUTURE

Six Months Later.

Holly hurried back from work after a stop at the supermarket to pick up her click-and-collect order. Angus was at training since the rugby season had started again after a break during December.

She was also back in netball training and had signed with the Dynamos for a second term. Hopefully, she'd be a consistent player in the starting team this year. That was the aim, at any rate.

But tonight, instead of heading to the gym for a session, she had a special mission. She dumped her box of groceries on the counter and made quick work of unpacking them. Dinner would be a Mexican soup, followed by pasta and decadent red velvet cakes presented in jars. Susan had put her on to the cakes. A woman named Grace made them, and they looked amazing.

After dinner, she'd put on music so they could dance together, and she'd tell Angus she loved him. Breathless and tingling with anticipation, Holly prepared their meal and set the table. She found a station playing romantic tunes and tore off to have a shower. Clothes—now there was a dilemma. She dithered between trousers and a dress and finally decided on a slim-fitting black dress that hit her mid-thigh.

The apartment door opened. "Holly, I'm home," Angus called.

Holly gave her hair a quick brush and stood. "I'm in here, Angus."

Angus appeared in the bedroom seconds later. He frowned. "Are we going out? Have I forgotten something?"

"No and no," Holly said with a smile. "I wanted to cook you a special dinner, and I thought I'd dress up too."

His gaze darkened as it slid over her. "You look gorgeous. Do I have time for a shower?"

"You do," she said and closed the distance between them. She beamed at him. "I love you, Angus O'Neil. You make me so happy."

His expression went blank before open pleasure and delight slid across his features. Their lips met in a ferocious kiss of passion and longing, arousal and hunger—pure love and enchantment.

"I love you in return, Holly Blackwood. These last months with you have been incredible."

"Thank you for your patience, your caring," Holly said. "You've shown me what a true partnership should be like, and I've never been happier. I truly love you. To the moon and back."

Angus grinned and kissed the tip of her nose. "I'll take that shower. Training was crazy tonight. I should've showered afterward, but I wanted to get home. Ten minutes," he promised.

Angus arrived in the kitchen dressed in black trousers and a blue shirt that brought out the sparkle in his eyes. He walked straight up to her at the stove where she was heating the soup. He stole a kiss and shunted the pot of soup off the heat.

"Angus, dinner is ready."

He took her hands and tugged, urging her to face him. "Holly, I love you. I'm crazy about you. Will you marry me?"

She gaped at him, and he nodded encouragement.

"Sweetheart, I'm asking if you'll marry me."

"Y-yes," she stuttered. "Yes!" she said more firmly.

Angus let out a whoop. He pulled the sapphire-and-diamond ring from his pocket and lifted her left hand to his mouth. He placed a kiss on her knuckles before he guided the band onto her finger. Then they were kissing again.

"You hijacked my special dinner," she murmured much later in the evening. Her stomach gave a protesting rumble.

"You surprised me," he countered with a grin. "I thought I'd surprise you, too. Now we have a story we can tell our kids."

"True," she agreed, and not even the thought of kids frightened her. She and Angus were a team, and they'd decide together when the time was right for a family.

Mid-morning, Clevedon

Holly watched Angus round the car to open the passenger door for her. He extended his hand, smiling, and gratitude filled her. How happy he made her, and she was grateful for second chances. She placed her left hand in his and stared at the shiny new sapphire-and-diamond ring adorning her finger.

"Are you nervous?" he asked.

"Petrified." An understatement. Her mother would go into instant wedding planning mode because Brooke had married without the rest of the family around. Maria would want to make up for that when Holly preferred no fuss and straightforward.

He smoothed his thumb over the ring, his expression full of tenderness. Love. Warmth suffused her, and she beamed at him, letting every overwhelming emotion show on her face.

"I like Clevedon," he said. "What would you think of the idea of buying a house here? One with a small block of land. We could have our base here during the off-season. The beach is close. It's near Connor's property and your parents, which means we'll have someone to monitor the place if we're out of town. It's a short drive from central Auckland and much quieter than the city."

"I love the idea. Fresh air. The piquant aroma of cow manure." She winked. "My parents would enjoy having us closer to home. They like you."

"I like them too." He glanced up at the front door of her parents' sprawling bungalow, and Holly followed his line of sight. A curtain twitched, and her parents and their fox terrier peeked out at them. "They're watching."

"Possibly wondering what's keeping us."

Angus drew her out of the car and pulled her close to sneak a kiss. The door opened behind them, and the scurry of feet indicated Bella had come to greet them. A chorus of barks from beside them had them pulling apart and laughing together.

Angus released her. "Are your parents going to be surprised?"

"Maria will have guessed already." Holly's phone burbled with an incoming call.

"Answer it," Angus said.

"I bet it's Brooke." Holly studied the number on the

screen and frowned. "It's not Brooke."

"Answer it," Angus repeated.

Holly stabbed the answer button. "Hello." She listened for a few minutes, a slow smile creeping across her face until she was grinning so wide her face hurt. "Thank you. Oh, thank you very much. Monday. Yes, okay. Thank you." She hung up in a daze, aware she'd babbled but too excited to care. "They've called me into the Silver Ferns. Their main defense player injured herself during training, and they need a reserve. Angus, I've made the team."

"Sweetheart, that's wonderful." He picked her up and swung her around, grinning broadly.

"What's going on out here?" her father demanded from the doorstep.

"Dad, the Silver Fern coach just called and asked me to attend the training camp."

Angus grabbed her for a long kiss, an exact repeat of the kiss she'd given him on learning he'd made the New Zealand rugby team to play Australia. When he finally lifted his head, he grinned and twined their fingers together. Hand-in-hand, they walked up the path to the front door, happiness making her feel as if she were floating.

"Congratulations, Holly," Maria said, bouncing in her excitement. "We're so proud of you."

"Well done," her father said in a gruff voice, grabbing her for a hug.

"Oh, my god," Maria shrieked. "Is that an engagement ring?"

Exhilaration widened Holly's beam. "That's what we came to tell you. Angus proposed last night. You're the first to know."

"Come inside," Maria said. "Oh, Holly. You look radiant. I don't have to ask if you're happy." Once inside, she gave Holly a hard hug and released her to do the same with Angus.

The dog jumped on Holly, wanting the same welcome. Bella's yip was demanding, and she turned in a tight circle. Holly crouched to scratch the brown-and-white animal behind its ears.

Her father shook Angus's hand, and his tough soldier-guy exterior cracked with a brief smile. Holly relaxed. Her father approved of her choice.

"I have a bottle of champagne in the car," Angus said. "I'll get it."

"I made the team," she said to her parents with a broad grin. "I report on Monday, and we're off to a training camp. I probably won't even play, but it's a toe in the door. It's a start."

"You've worked hard," her father said. "You deserve this."

"An engagement, too," Maria gushed. "This is so exciting. You'll have the wedding here in Clevedon."

"Yes, Mum," Holly said. "After Angus gets back from

tour and the netball season ends."

"Excellent. Plenty of time to plan." Maria rubbed her hands together.

"A small wedding," Holly said, her tone decisive. To her relief, Maria nodded and bustled away to get glasses.

"Are you happy, Holly?" her father asked in his gruff manner.

"Yes. So happy. Angus is perfect for me, Dad."

"As long as he treats you well."

"He does. Angus is wonderful."

Angus came inside with the bottle of chilled champagne and poured four glasses.

The bubbles tickled Holly's nose as she took a quick sip. Then she raised her glass in a toast. "To love and sport."

"Congratulations," her father said.

"To love and sport," Maria echoed, bouncing on her toes. "We're so proud of you both."

"To successful games," Angus said, his gaze locking with Holly's, then he mouthed, "I love you."

Holly grinned through misty tears, thankful for second chances and this man who completed her in the best of ways. She stepped up beside him and linked their hands. Together, they were a winning team.

WANT A PEEK AT Angus's and Holly's Future?

Not quite ready to let Angus and Holly go? Me neither. Subscribe to my newsletter, and receive a copy of the bonus story: *Dreams Come True*

VISIT THIS LINK
(www.subscribepage.com/sportslovers_bonus)
to subscribe and receive your free bonus story.

If you enjoyed this sports romance, you might like Blindside, (www.shelleymunro.com/books/blindside) which features a rugby-playing heroine.

ABOUT AUTHOR

USA Today bestselling author Shelley Munro lives in Auckland, the City of Sails, with her husband and a cheeky Jack Russell/mystery breed dog.

Typical New Zealanders, Shelley and her husband left home for their big OE soon after they married (translation of New Zealand speak - big overseas experience). A twelve-month-long adventure lengthened to six years of roaming the world. Enduring memories include being almost sat on by a mountain gorilla in Rwanda, lazing on white sandy beaches in India, whale watching in Alaska, searching for leprechauns in Ireland, and dealing with ghosts in an English pub.

While travel is still a big attraction, these days Shelley

is most likely found in front of her computer following another love - that of writing stories of contemporary and paranormal romance and adventure. Other interests include watching rugby (strictly for research purposes), cycling, playing croquet and the ukelele, and curling up with an enjoyable book.

Visit Shelley at her Website
www.shelleymunro.com

Join Shelley's Newsletter
www.shelleymunro.com/newsletter

OTHER BOOKS BY SHELLEY

Fancy Free

Protection

Romp

Buzz

Festive

Friendship Chronicles

Secret Lovers

Reunited Lovers